BECKETT'S TREASURE

A DEBUTANT'S MYSTERY

Anita K. Mills

BECKETT'S TREASURE
A DEBUTANT'S MYSTERY

Published in the United Kingdom

First Printing, 2021

:

TABLE OF CONTENTS

Acknowledgements

Thanks to Teresa Beeler of Breckenridge Crossing for all her help.

Disclaimer

Any references to historical events, real people or real places are used fictitiously. Names, characters and places are products of the author's imagination.

CHAPTER ONE

The Death of a Sergeant
Monday, 19th March 1849

My name is Catherine Brentwood, or Katie, to my friends. I am eighteen and the younger sister of three brothers; two natural, one adopted, and one younger sister.

I am normally a bright eyed, intelligent and happy young woman, who clamours for the next mystery novel that I can find, but today I am a little subdued and with good reason. Now, I have a true-life unhappy mystery of my own to puzzle out.

I am sitting in the small armchair in my parent's sitting room at Brentwood House on the River Thames, wearing the conventional black as I have just returned from church. My parents, along with Lord and Lady Catsford and Sir Walter and Hilary Kettering, have retired for a rest upstairs before lunch. My guests therefore, as the eldest daughter it is my job to be hostess, are Captain John

Beckett, Sergeant Davis Kettering, Sergeant Andrew Catsford and his wife Margaret, and Corporal Steven Etterwood.

Opening a small leather-bound book that I have just withdrawn from my pocket; I wait until all have a drink and a seat before I speak. It did not take long.

"We found this in his kitbag that arrived last week from the Tower of London Barracks with the usual condolences from the top brass. So, if you have time, I'd like to summarise the last few entries?"

I looked at each of my brother's best friends and each one responded with a nod.

"This is one of his journals that he always had with him while he was away. He inscribed the inside flap with: Sergeant Peter Brentwood. Kandy Barracks Ceylon. Green Howards, Yorkshire Regiment, Richmond Barracks, North Yorkshire. On loan from The Royal Fusiliers (City of London Regiment) Tower of London Barracks. It runs from the 1st of July 1848 to 1st February 1849, but I will start on Friday, 31st January 1849 as this is where it gets interesting."

I looked down and focused on the words that Peter had written as I read them aloud.

'I have had enough, not only of the fighting, but being here in Kandy Barracks. Last Spring, The Sikh War in India began with the deaths of two young men; Patrick Vans Agnew and Lieutenant William Anderson. The army sent them to Multan with instructions to oversee the exchange of the governor, who wanted to be relieved and hand it over to his successor. On this mission, Agnew, who worked for East India Company and Lieutenant William Anderson of the Bombay Army, required the last six years financial reports. While they waited, they inspected the Multan Fort. But on the way back, adherents of Mulraj, who had gone over to the enemy, brutally attacked and murdered them.

Was the attack prearranged? But why? Because of the financial reports not stacking up, or because someone wanted Agnew or Anderson out of the way? Curious.

This incident caused a profound sensation throughout India. All liked both the murdered officers and mourned them publicly. Agnew's death, in particular, was tough. In private, they stated he was brave, modest, and unselfish. He had won the esteem and affection of all who knew him. I met him once, liked him, and totally agreed with that assessment. The war went on.'

I paused and glanced up at my attentive audience. "Now I will read the next part about The Matale Rebellion," I instructed my brother's friends.

'The Kandyan provinces were in a state of turmoil, even though they had been under British rule for some thirty years. Britain had no business being there. They did not know how to run another country with a different climate and putting British rule on to a people who were just coming to terms without one. This was downright ludicrous. Plus, bringing in a new crop for the country to grow as well as slave labour to work the land was even worse. This country grew mostly tea and knew not of other crops.

In the 1830s, the British introduced coffee into Ceylon- Sri-Lanka, a crop which flourishes in high altitudes, and grown on the land taken from the peasants. Therefore, the decline in coffee production in the West Indies, where it came from, and with the abolition of slavery there, caused trouble in Ceylon. So, with the peasants and the slaves, the two countries were in chaos and all brought about by British rule or more likely from The East India Company that was under British rule.

However, the dispossessed peasantry did not work on the plantations, but were not as dumb as the British made them out to be. Kandyan villagers refused to abandon their traditional subsistence holdings and become wage-workers in the nightmarish conditions that prevailed on these new estates, despite all the pressure exerted by the colonial state. The British, therefore, had to draw on its army of reserve labour in India to man its lucrative new outpost to the south. The infamous system of contract labour now established, which transported hundreds of thousands of Tamil 'coolies' from southern India into Sri Lanka for the coffee estates.

These Tamil labourers died in tens of thousands both on the journey itself and on the plantations and they weren’t the only ones. I lost fellow soldiers to all kinds of diseases. Being this close to each other, everyone got dysentery in one form or another. The Tamils were never more than two feet away at any given time. They ate near us, even from our own cook house, and some even volunteered to help with the cooking. Luckily, it was only one day's sea voyage, so I ate the dry biscuits they rationed us with. Therefore, I had no food from the cook's house today.

And that's how I got here. Shipped over from India, but nothing seems different. I enlisted because they offered me three square meals a day, plus a decent bed and got neither. The job came with disease, though I was lucky, it seems to have passed me by and planting of holes. They talk of latrines, but I'm sure they meant bullet holes, if you weren't lucky.

Though I wash my hands with carbolic soap, that I'm sent from my cousin, Daniel, who owns the soap factory in London. He told me to wash every meal time and whenever I use the bathroom, and I use the term loosely as bathrooms are few and far between either in India or here in Sri-Lanka, and always stand sideways, so not to get shot at. Up to now, both bits of advice seem to work? So, I taught my three best friends this trick and they too get soap sent to them from home and stand sideways when shooting, or lay down, said Davis, with a laugh, which works equally well. Captain Beckett seems to use the same tactics. Decent fellow must have him round for a drink when back at home again.

Because of an economic depression in England that had affected most of the country, along with a recent food shortage, not to mention the work prospects of a newly left scholar, I enlisted with starry eyes of conquering far off exotic countries, not squalid ones that were as bad as England. This depression was severely affecting the coffee and cinnamon industry to a degree that the planters and merchants clamoured for a reduction of export duties.

Sir James Emerson Tennent, the Colonial Secretary in Colombo, recommended to Earl Grey, Secretary of State for the Colonies in London, that taxation should radically shift from indirect taxation to direct taxation and they accepted the proposal. They abolished the export duty on coffee and reduced the export duty on cinnamon, leaving a deficit of £40,000 Sterling per annum, which was to be met by direct taxes on, you guessed it, the people.

You hear a lot when on duty. The 'top brass' may have approved this, but the people certainly did not.

Queen Victoria dispatched a new governor, 35-year-old Lord Torrington and a cousin of the Prime Minister, Lord Russell, to Colombo to carry out these reforms.

I arrived on 1 July 1848, and on that day, license fees imposed on guns, dogs, carts, shops and labour were made compulsory on plantation roads. Well, everything really, but the people, unless you paid a special tax. These taxes bore heavily, not only on the purse but also on the traditions of the Kandyan peasant. Therefore, as I expected, a mass movement against the oppressive taxes was developing. I could see it, but the Lieutenant

General Charles Turner either had gone blind, or he was told to ignore it. The masses were without the deposed leadership of their native King, or their chiefs, who the British crushed after the Uva Rebellion or were collaborating with the colonial power and who the people now distrusted and hated, or so we were told. They did not like us either.

The leadership passed for the first time in the Kandyan provinces into the hands of ordinary people and when the people had a lot more to lose than their lives, well, anything can happen and it did on 26th July 1848 through The Rebellion.

The rebels attacked government buildings, including those in Matale, and destroyed some of the tax records and that's where I came in with the army to put down the rebellion.

While fighting broke out in the Kandy streets, other places too were fighting where the British Army shot eight people dead. We obtained no casualties.

Governor Torrington immediately declared Martial Law on 29th July 1848 in Kandy and on 31st July in Kurunegala.

The British troops took one leader prisoner and executed him on 8th August. The others went into hiding and lived in a cave, 13 kilometres (8.1 miles) from Matale.

Torrington issued a warrant for their arrest with a reward of £150 for information on his whereabouts. Though every soldier here could have done with the money, Torrington declared that if any man left the barracks, he would declare him absent without leaving and they would shoot him on sight.

I knew there was more to this than a reward. I was sure.

They caught two men outside and within two days, held in strict incommunicado, they shot them. Their bodies shipped back to England, or so we were told.

Weird things: I was on guard duty and I never heard the shots and when I asked in the barracks about the two men, no one seemed to know who they were? But it doesn't pay to ask questions in Kandy. Just ask its two reporters, oh wait, the British executed them for spreading propaganda lies.

On 21st September 1848, Malaysian soldiers arrested Gongalegoda Banda, the leader, though he offered resistance before his arrest. They transported him from Matale to Kandy, where they held him prisoner. Why are Malaysian soldiers here; three nations, one job? Bit of an overkill, again, unless there was more than just the three watching their own property.

The trial of the leader Gongalegoda Banda began on 27th November at the Supreme Court sessions in Kandy. They charged him with high treason for claiming to be King of Kandy and waging war against the British. I thought they were after the East India Company for the theft of their land. He declared he was guilty of all the charges. The Supreme Court condemned him to be hanged on 1st January 1849.

I was on guard duty at the courthouse. I do not know who the man was I saw talking to the judge, but he did not look British or Kandyan. Swiss, maybe? And the Judge did not appear happy.

Subsequently, command issued a proclamation within the hour to amend the death sentence to flogging a hundred times and deportation to Malaysia. Why to Malaysia? This was just getting too much. The Malaysian army carried out the sentence that afternoon, behind closed doors, yet watched by the leader of EIC. The Malaysian army took the man away on a stretcher the next morning. Something clearly did not add up.

The Matale Rebellion was over and the leaders; dead or in prison. This completed our job and frankly, the entire regiment had seen enough. We finished our time here, and the army was sending us home, back to England, to the Richmond Barracks in North Yorkshire. After that, we'll head home to the Tower of London Barracks for some rest and relaxation. Personally, I could not wait, but somehow, I knew both these two incidents were related and more was? were to come.

Thursday, 1st February

I did not want to play cards on my last night, even with my best friends, so I went for a walk, but later, I wished I had.

After the last tent, I stopped and lit up. It was my first cigarette of the day and I was looking forward to it, only I did not know it would be my last here. Mum says I had to quit; it wasn't healthy to smoke.

But I'd been here seven months in this living hell and smoking helped. As I watched the last dregs of the sun as she slowly disappeared into the lake that separated the barracks and the town itself and wondering what home would be like after two years away, I happily smoked the last half of the cigarette.

I had not been there long when I could hear hushed tones coming from the last tent. They were not loud enough to hear what was being said, but enough to recognise the voice of one; Grimy or Captain Oliver Grimshaw. I did not like the man, yet I could not state why. He seemed to be agitated with the conversation, and he became a little louder in his agitation. I stepped closer. They were only a few scattered words, but they got this sergeant's attention. *Treasure, Ruin, and Brentwood.* I was sure they weren't talking about me. Though Grimy and I had our run-ins over the past two years.

"A lot?" inquired Grimshaw.

"Yes," replied the other.

"Yeah, right, what do you take me for?"

"No, it's absolutely true. Belongs to Thomas À Becket, Archbishop of Canterbury, no less. But if you breathe a word of this, it will find us in a ditch with no voice boxes, okay?"

There was a silence, so I assumed Grim was nodding.

I knew my classics and my history and thought, did Thomas ever go to Brentwood? Unknown, but he travelled extensively during his life, including to France, so he could have.

Treasure, eh, I thought, smiling. Why *not me and mine?* I saw the tent flap open, and a man stepped out. He was light haired, older than I, but thinner. His uniform, though I did not recognise it, was slightly off. John's uniform was more, I don't know, it could be an old one. I knew the new uniforms for commissioned officers were changing, but didn't realize they were already in use. I turned in the opposite direction, so he did not see who I was, in case he thought I had overheard and hoping they had not noticed me. Hurrying back to my tent, I wanted to make notes of what I had heard, but I knew they had followed me. I will go back outside shortly to see if I can find my tail and follow him. Wonder if it was Grim? Maybe he could tell me more with a little persuasion.

I will replace my journal back in my kitbag in its secret compartment and will add to it when I can.'

I closed the Journal as I sucked in a large breath and looked up at my wide-eyed audience. "Grimy was sure up to something, but what? What do you make of that?" I asked.

"Good job. My leave is indefinite, and I've brought an extra bag of clothes. I will stay if I may? There's more to this, I'm sure." Stated the captain with a shrug.

He was a tall man, around thirty-five, with broad shoulders, dark brown hair, brown eyes and a northern accent. He always seemed to think before he spoke. Educated at oxford and spent two years abroad before joining the Army. I knew a lot about my brother's friends. Captain Beckett had escorted both me and my mother, as my father had not been well that day, to Margaret and Andrew's wedding as James, as usual, was running late.

"I'd like to know who offered him three square meals a day? The army doesn't and you're lucky if you get one or a bed?" The captain continued, but he did not laugh.

"Do you have a room for us too, Katie? We should investigate this. I knew there was more to it," replied Margaret, "and I'll ask my brother to come around early. He's just got off a murder case and well, exhausted it seems, so they sent him home to Devon for a couple of days R and R. His observation might be useful."

I had known Margaret (or Mags) and her family for a long time. She was tall, thin and delicate, yet possessed a sharp as a knife intelligence. Blue eyes, blond shoulder length hair and rarely talked much. We had met at school and had become good friends. Our families had met because of that friendship and our mothers had become firm in their own friendship, too. It was through me and Peter that she had met Andrew Catsford and fell in love.

Andrew is a tall, long legged athletic man who enjoyed his sports. He too was blond haired and blue eyed. Jovial and a merry soul, my mother called him. Our families were close because he and Peter had gone through school and college as well as sat their sergeants' exams together, which pleased both our families when they passed. They could have bought themselves in, but Peter always wanted to 'start at the bottom and climb high quickly', a satisfying way to live.

The Catsfords owned the Whitewood Estate in Devon, along with a town house here in London's Governor Square. Both places close to ours and they had just come from Devon for Pete's funeral. Both Andrew and Davis' parents were also upstairs keeping mother company. Davis was the elder of the four by almost a year. Like Andrew and Peter, he was at the same school and college.

They all three loved rowing and one day, Peter had told her, they didn't have enough for a crew when up popped this tall lanky dark-haired boy, who said tell me what to do and I'll do it. Not wishing to forgo the chance of being out on the river, they took him on board and Davis became the third of 'the cads.' Not much of a nickname, but it stuck. All knew Pete as Curious Peter because he always wanted to know more, hence Cads.

Last year, Mags came out. They introduced her to the Princess no less, but Andy had already spoken to his father, who spoke to Sir Frank and Mirabel Hampshire, and the families agreed on nuptials. Pete had been Andy's best man, and Davis and Steven had been his ushers. Though Steven was not as tall as the others or as old, yet they all treated him like a younger brother.

Corporal Steven Etterwood was black haircd, with brown eyes and a small, yet robust physique. They had gone from Cads to Beck's Lot to Captain Beckett's Knights.

Steven had lived at our house ever since his parents had died almost ten years ago. My father went to his school and while there on an inspection, the school took him to the infirmary to find a lad with a knee injury. What the school doctor was doing to the lad shocked him, so much so he took over. Not a man to reproach, he got a junior doctor from the hospital to go to the school to help the doctor under his authority. In the meantime, he found the boy had no parents, was well to do with an enormous fortune, when he turned twenty-one and a trust was running his life; rather poorly. They sent him to a mediocre school and were pocketing the difference as well as dipping into the money whenever they liked. Within a month, through my father's attention, Steven's fortune and inheritance was safe under father's bank of trustees and the adoption papers signed. His knee healed quickly, too.

Therefore, Steven Etterwood Brentwood was now a member of the family. He had entered school with both Peter and James though a few years behind and then joined up the week after leaving college and joined Peter, Davis and Andrew's Regiment. They had all been away together since Autumn 46' first at college, then to India, then later, Ceylon. Though we hoped not, yet knew, they all could die; yet no one expected Pete's death to be murder.

They had all come to the funeral from the barracks, some with a three-day pass, which now may look to be longer. I was thankful I had all the beds turned this morning. My mother would not hear of them going anywhere else.

I was afraid the death of my brother would make my father ill again, but James, my eldest brother, a student doctor, following in my father's footsteps, was upstairs with him. He was taking care and watching for any signs of deterioration, along with my youngest sister, Mary. So far there was only exhaustion from going to church.

"Will Gregory be all right?" I asked, alarmed, coming back to Margret.

I liked Detective Gregory Hampshire of the North London Police Force. He helped put me right if I got the wrong clue that led me to the wrong bad guy in my novels. He got it right every time. An uncanny knack at that, my father had said on one of his good days, well suited to detecting.

"We hope so." replied Margaret. "Just needs to rest and some fresh air. His doctor advised a few days at most. He was in Devon with mother and father," she added. "They could not come for the funeral as mother cannot travel with her broken hip. But where Gregory is now, I don't know. Mother said he left Friday. I'll go around to his apartment this afternoon."

I nodded, relieved. All here had connections to Devon, one way or another. Our family home was near Devizes, that James was now running as well as continuing his training at London hospital. While father was on leave from the palace because of being ill, James was watching over him and had an interview at the local Lunatic Asylum tomorrow. If my father did not recover in that time, the palace and the medical board would choose another. Then James would officially become Lord Brentwood. It had almost been six months since father became ill, but because of Peter's death, the board had extended father's absence. Lord Forester had been to see father on Friday, and he worried he may never be well enough to continue his practice and James was nowhere near enough trained to take over.

“Tell us again what you saw, Steve?” Asked Andy, leaning forward from the settee. “I still can't get my head around it.”

“Well, as I stated at the inquest, I came out of my tent to find Pete standing near his. There was another man with his back to me, but he was blonde, different uniform too. Then, suddenly, he was running. I too, began running as I watched Pete fall to the ground. As I arrived and fell to my knees beside Pete, I called for the other to stop. But the other kept going. I lost him as I was now below the tent line so could not see him anymore. ‘Tired,’ Pete said, ‘tell my family I love them. I’ll be waiting, don't let me down baby brother.’ he finished, then he closed his eyes. I swear I did everything I could, but I’m not a medic. There was so much blood. The bearers came and carried him away, yet I swear Pete died in my arms.” His face had lost all its colour.

I reached over and held his arm. I had been copying his statement into Pete’s journal, as there were plenty of unused pages. Maybe once we have found the person responsible for his death, then the book could be closed.

I whispered when Steve had finished. “The coroner’s report…,” my lips quivered as I spoke, and Steve pressed my hand on his arm and gave me a small smile of encouragement, so I continued. "He declared it to be an unlawful killing. That someone used a thin-bladed knife and pushed it hard into his left lung. Death followed within minutes. And Steve, even if you had been a battlefield doctor, you could not have saved him. James went through the report finely and told me so. The killer knew where to strike and did. Peter had no chance. But what James and I want to know is the who and the why?"

"And we will." Put in John. "First, we need information on Grimshaw. Hopefully, he knows who the killer is and then we should know the why."

"What happened to Pete's Brunswick rifle, he was a marksman. A sharpshooter. He never put it down except to sleep and he had it when he left us?" Steven asked. "I did not see that guy pick it up and run off with it, though my eyes were on Pete at the time."

Andrew and Davis agreed.

"I'll ask tomorrow," replied John.

"And about the blade, I did not think it was army issue."

"Was he right?" I asked, "About it being Brentwood the place, not my brother?"

"Again, only Oliver Grimshaw can answer that question," Replied John. "Steve, maybe you and I will nip back to the Orange Street Barracks tomorrow and see if we can find him. Maybe have a quiet word inside the officer's mess, with a friend of mine." He paused for a moment before adding. "There is nothing in the tale of treasure of Beckets in Brentwood, though that's always puzzled me as they flock there every year looking for it. Henry the Second placed a witch hunt order on my ancestor, you know. My ancestor's brother-in-law, Thomas Beckett, my line, stated that he believed the Knights of Henry had specific orders to get rid of Thomas and he paid handsomely for it. The Knights kept all their wealth, lands, and titles that were passed down to their sons, even after the courts convicted them, which is most unusual. My ancestor's family helped bring the Knights to justice and kept a vigil on his burial site, for a long time in case Henry's followers tried to desecrate it. It's all in my family records. Though my parents raised me in north Nottingham, our family estates are actually in Brentwood. So, I know all there is to know of Becket's chapel there, but I'm absolutely sure there was never any mention of any kind of treasure attached to it. I'm sure my family would have dug it up five minutes after they buried it and spent it." He laughed softly. "So, this is the short version. Brentwood began as a clearing made in the woods by burning trees (hence 'burnt wood' which became Brentwood. Brent being the Middle English at the time for burnt) to provide a stop-off point about one day's journey from the Thames for pilgrims en route from East Anglia to the shrine of Thomas Becket at Canterbury. The first church building dedicated to St Thomas in Brentwood was a chapel built around 1221 to serve these pilgrims. Ruins of this original Chapel of St Thomas à Becket, with its walls of irregular ragstone and flint, are still to be seen in the High Street.

The Augustinian Abbey of St Osyth founded the chapel, near Colchester, and it stood within the small town established by the abbey alongside the Colchester to London Road. They intended it as a chapel of ease, for the use of the inhabitants of the town and for travellers and pilgrims on the route to Canterbury. However, as a subsidiary chapel to South Weald Church some two-and-a-half miles to the north west, it could only hold divine offices on the dedicatory saint's day and at the time of the charter fair after 1227. They substantially rebuilt the chapel in the 14th century. In this, its last form, which was illustrated in 1843, the building included a rectangular nave and smaller rectangular chancel, with a tower in the north-west corner and a narrow porch on the north side. The building continued its use as a chapel until 1832; thereafter, it housed the Boys National School." John paused and held up an index finger as he stated, "This is where history differs. The second chapel of St Thomas 1835, built on a Nursery Garden, South of high street, a mile or so from the original, which was reached by a path on the line of St Thomas Road. Originally gated at the town's end and with the opening of the town's railway in 1840, the town immediately expanded farther southwards towards the station, and by 1844 they laid out the Queen's Road and New Road.

By 1848, they had built a steam mill and one hundred new houses, giving work to the town. Now this all led away from the old first Chapel; Gresham Road and Rose Valley, where my family's seat is. They built the Manor house there soon after the first chapel. And there was a path that led from the manor to the family chapel. So, the family then could travel not only in safety but also not with the town's people or the pilgrims, either. There, along that path, was a lodge that the family could rest in, but on the day that the knights attacked Thomas, it caught fire and burnt to the ground.

Coincident? No one knows. There was a small rhyme that started up soon after.

'Burnt Lodge, Burnt Wood.
Thomas dead, no more he could preach.
His riches go with him to teach.
Burnt Lodge, Burnt Wood, his soul and
his beech.'

This is the strange part, so my family records state. Thomas never stayed in the lodge when he visited, he only stayed at the manor. Yet many have come looking and it was this tourist trade that helped the town grow, but not alone. It's said the opening of the Essex Regiment Barracks in 1843 stimulated the expansion, though in Warley, the government sold the barrack's there to the East India Company. Then in 1849, they started building the Warley Hospital and shortly to follow the Essex Lunatic Asylum which the town's major houses already funded. My father's is one, but when my father asked for warrantee of why; he was told because of the size of the town. My father replied the amount of people is two thousand and still far lower than the town of Romford. 'Orders' he was told."

"So, there's the East India Company again?" I added. "Old English, your rhyme, by the way and beech, means book. Burnt lodge in Brentwood, Thomas dead, no more he could preach, his riches go with him. Burnt Lodge, Burnt Wood, his soul and his beech. His Beech would be his bible. Did he leave his bible with you?"

"No, but there is a plaque on one wall stating 'Burntwood Chapel of Thomas à Becket.' Strange. There is no actual connection to the Archbishop of Canterbury except the shrine, which was built long after his death. No one ever called to visit his sister and his brother-in-law to pay their respects or to offer their condolences, and Thomas only came twice in his life. Too busy he reported to dally." John's hand raised and rubbed at the back of his neck, thinking of his next words.

He continued to explain, "There's the London-Colchester ride, a coach service with three daily coaches, that stops at the White Hart inn and a wagon service four times a week. There's also a lodge near to the chapel in Western Road, or bed and breakfasts on the north road. Though, I'd stay clear of those if I were you. There are inns all over, but one called Robin Hood on Onger Road, which the local college inhabit followed by a few more on High Road. I don't think we need to make a high-profile visit, do you, if we go? After all, they often recommend visiting the country after the death of a relative, do they not?"

They all nodded their heads, including me.

"The crown," he continued, "though adjoins the second chapel and history says there's a secret passage between the two, but they shut it in 1818. A dangerous building, they claim. The Marquis of Grandy sits across the road."

"Any relation of my uncle's?" laughed Davis. "Probably, on my mother's side, of course."

"Unknown," said the captain with a smirk.

"This town seems to house far more inns, than most of the big towns?" The corporal laughed, shaking his head.

"Thirsty town, indeed," replied Andrew.

"There is also a police station on Coptford Road." stated the captain.

"Nice to know, is that just in case." Chuckled Andy, although slightly subdued.

"Why," said Margaret, changing the subject back to Peter. "… does Pete talk about Kandy Barracks and the Town's Rebellion? Could that have anything to do with his death? He did nose a bit. Best be thorough!" she added.

John thought for a moment. "We need more information and Grimshaw still holds the key. I never looked beyond what I was doing, but Pete always took an interest in the local area. He did the same in India before they shipped us to Ceylon. But I remember the two men, the soldiers, who were supposed to be flogged for being outside the barracks the night after Torrenton's statement was told to us and we, the captains, had to inform the rest of the men. They never explained why they were outside, or so we were told. Instead of a court hearing and flogging, they executed them at dawn two days later and I believe Peter was on guard duty then."

I stood. "Well, as you say, John, Grimshaw holds the key. So, until he's questioned, we are in the dark and twiddling our thumbs. I'll see how long lunch is going to be." I walked out the door, conscious of many pairs of eyes on my back.

CHAPTER TWO

James Brentwood and a Shock at Hanley
Tuesday, 20 March 1849

Hanley Lunatic Asylum, London

Though I felt wretched and I certainly did not feel like working, I stopped the carriage in the grounds close to the gates of Hanley Lunatic Asylum, where my next half term was to take place, for my interview. Though I had done my general training for two years at London Hospital in general medicine, the crazies had always fascinated me since I began my training. I sat thinking of this while I waited to see the head consultant.

My father is a doctor and my grandfather before him, so it was only natural being the eldest son to follow in their footsteps, that's not to say I don't like it, I do. My maternal family was in the forces. So, Pete and I agreed, he would go into the army as tradition and I would go to Medical School. Though little good it's done me, Pete's dead, and no one seems to care, but our immediate family and close friends. Though my sister Catherine is taking this well, my parents and younger sister are not. It's a lot to put on her young shoulders, especially when this year was her coming out season. It should have been full of dancing, having fun, and spotting the man who is to be her husband. But with the loss of Peter, she's put it on hold until next year. Mary has at least another two, hopefully. Personally, I hate the Marriage Markets, but I too will use it to find a suitable 'Lady of Brentwood.'

With John looking into my brother's death through the army side, I was hoping he would come up with something to explain the coroner's report that I read cover to cover and did not understand how it could have happened. But hopefully between us, we are sure we could come up with a reason why my brother is dead. Though he did not die on a battlefield, instead in a knife attack on the barracks field, apparently by one of his own and with almost five thousand other soldiers around him. Yet no one saw anything other than Steven. It just makes little sense! I could not get it out of my mind.

"Hm," said the consultant. "Are you with me, Mister Brentwood?"

I apologised to Doctor Harfield for my lack of concentration and gave him the reason.

"I sympathise as I too have lost a brother to the Battlefield, though not the same, I agree, and share the feeling of loss."

I nodded and thanked him.

"Well, maybe that's what this lesson can be of today. Seven years have elapsed since the experiment of 'non-restraint' has been fully tried here in the Hanley Asylum. Doctor Connelly, in the spirit of Christian philosophy, started this, and it's easier on both staff and inmates. We have forty-three patients here at the moment, but we have had less and more over the years.

Though many soldiers die on the battle field, a lot do not, yet they are never the same. They cannot ease back into society and expect to carry on after the horrors seen and felt. Some even end up here. We are currently housing twenty-three that are soldiers, ten females and a further ten males, three of them from the docks.

Most are over eighteen, though we have a tragic case of a twelve-year-old boy who killed his father, with mitigating circumstances. The father had beaten him since he was two, especially after a skin full. Usually, they grow up to be drinkers and beaters too, as they know no other way. In this case, though, the boy turned as the father went for the boy's mother. He hasn't stopped stabbing his father, even without the knife or the body. The poor wretch falls into exhaustive sleep only to get up and continue his fight. Shamefully, the father survived and will walk away.

Of the twenty-three soldiers, most are drink related, but two are not. These two lost it on the battlefield and killed a few of their own side before their fellow soldiers stopped them. Their cases are similar to a term we call 'Blood Rage,' but they are unrelated. Different wars, different regiments, different backgrounds, yet housed next door to each other, they seem to talk to each other. Soldiers' pay was nominally one shilling per day, but "stoppages" of up to sixpence (half a shilling) decreased this for their daily rations. Other stoppages occurred for replacement clothing, damages, medical services and so on. In 1847, they laid it down that a soldier must receive at least one penny per day, regardless of all stoppages.

My brother's pay was for six years and twenty-one days, excluding food, kit, clothing and disciplinary action on three occasions and any medical treatment, which turned out was 365 pennies per year timed by six plus 21, which equals 2,211. My mother received half that amount, and she had to pay for his burial costs. They don't half getaway with things."

I nodded. "We've only received his kitbag so far, but that was half empty."

"War really does not help the mental wellbeing of a soldier. Put that together with drink and you have a very sick soldier on your hands that could turn dangerous. Sometimes, they could turn against his own or inward and shut down, getting himself killed and maybe two or more around him killed as well. Some end up here. I'll show you."

We left the office and strolled down the corridor. The entire building was of white glazed bricks, except for one line of bricks painted dark blue about five feet off the ground. We followed the blue line down to the lifts. When we cranked the lift, it creaked noisily down to the next level, where Harfield continued his description of the facility.

"We house six here, on this level of which there are two. We classify this level as grade one.

They will neither self-harm nor harm another. Up to now, the Mental Asylum has had a poor reputation, but I, through Doctor Connelly's work with the help of a few others, want to change that reputation with a new and humane attitude towards mental healthcare. Here at Hanley, we are setting standards for others to follow and support from the government is helping to change the old view.

The word Asylum comes from institutions run by monks or priests which they provided asylum for everyone who asked for it. In other words, a refuge. Before asylums, people with mental health problems or learning disabilities stayed at home and family cared for them, but it was a close call whether or not they survived. Deaths deemed accidental are at least now being questioned. Christmas time was especially hard as the mental patients disrupted so much of the festivities that thoughts of 'charity begins at home' were completely forgotten.

So, doctors commissioned places like a Lunatic Asylum for those who could not remain at home and the families could not afford to put them into hospitals. Though many often ended up destitute, begging for food and shelter on the street. In the 1700s, there were a few private institutions where wealthy families could send their 'Mad' relatives to be cared for with discretion. The poor had to rely on local parishes, which sometimes provided charity-funded asylums, but most either ended up in workhouses, prisons, or died of starvation and cold on the streets."

We came to the first door, marked with the

number one. Here the consultant paused.

"Mr Jeffery Saltash came to us last year as he does not recognise himself or those close to him. Apparently, he went to bed fine one night, but the next morning, screamed the place down, wanting someone called Margery, but there is no one called Margery living in the house. Nothing or no one could calm him. They called me in to consult and I was curious, so I brought him here with his family's consent to see if I can make a change. Through the year, we have made progress to the point he goes home once a week to sleep, but he still wants his wife called Margery and sobs every night."

We turned to the room across the corridor. Room Two said the plaque.

"Now this case is unique. A young lady completely catatonic, but not mad, terrified, maybe."

This time, he unlocked the door.

"Miss Samantha Danvers came…"

I stumbled back against the wall, and Doctor Harfield quickly turned and held me up against the corridor wall. After a moment, his assistant, who had followed, held me while the doctor relocked the door. With the aid of his assistant, they took me back to his office and given a chair with the waiting arrival of some freshly brewed tea.

He waited till I was ready. Quite concerned.

"Forgive me," I murmured, "but the lady in question is none other than my second cousin, who should have arrived Sunday, stayed the night and come with the family to my brother's funeral. My sister, Catherine is riding over today to her house to find out why she never arrived."

"I see," said the doctor, pouring the boiled water from the kettle into the pot sitting by the small Bunsen burner and a metal plate on legs.

"Being mentally ill is one of the worst illnesses to treat. Ninety-nine percent of people that are brought into an asylum leave later in a coffin; the rest never see the outside world again. I am afraid there is no happy ending for the 'crazies.' They are just too tightly imbibed in their fantasy world. Maybe they don't want to be released, maybe they are so 'happy' being there that the body slowly dies because it's not attended to, who knows. It's sad, but it's reality."

I nodded. "I realise that. My friend, Anthony Stable, had a sister who they admitted into an asylum and she just deteriorated until she passed away last month. There was nothing they could do. My friend begged my help. So, I went to see the girl. Force feeding her did not work. Threats or any other force did not work, so she slowly faded from lack of food and died within a year. So very sad. I felt so helpless that I could not help. My friend called me useless, what good was I as a doctor or as a friend and I agreed. I needed to know more."

"Hence the reason you're on this circuit of one stop learning. Very few take this road, very few see that point of view. MDs only learn enough to treat a wound, then send them to specialists when the case warrants, but even specialists are narrow in their fields and don't look at the bigger picture. Here, we try to see that bigger picture and treat the whole person, not just the mental process. Maybe your second cousin could be your first case."

I nodded.

"Instead of waiting until next week, why don't you start tomorrow, if you think you are recovered enough."

I nodded again. The tea had certainly revived me, and the wonder of how my cousin got here.

"Okay, here's her file. Read it over this evening and return it to me in the morning either by hand or messenger before nine with your answer. Does it sound like something that you could relate to? Help make a change and bring us into the new world of medicine."

I did like the idea and told Doctor Harfield that I had a lot of thinking and research to do. We talked a little more about my cousin and then I thanked him for my morning at Hanley. I thought I would be eager to start my full day tomorrow. We shook hands, and I left and drove the carriage home, deep in thought.

So, I had my first case. Who would have believed it would be my second cousin. I could not wait to read how she ended up in Hanley.

I arrived home at twelve-thirty promptly and caught my sister going into the sitting room while she awaited the lunch hour. "Catherine, I wonder if tomorrow would you accompany me to Hanley at eight." I asked calmly.

"What, fed up with me already, brother?" She teased lightly.

"What, oh yes, very droll sister, but no. There's a patient that they just admitted, married only a week…"

“Wow,” she interrupted. “He got to know her quick.”

“Yes, very. Too quick for my liking.

“I don't think she’s in the least bit crazy, but terrified. She sure could do with a friend, hoping you would get the girl to talk, as no male can get close without her screaming. It's possible they have molested her in some terrifying way? But no one is sure. No one has got close to her, and she doesn’t seem to like the nurses they have.” I chuckled, “I don't blame her, they give me the shivers.”

“James,” she chided, then laughed shortly. She gave me the desired answer, of course. “Brother, I’ll be ready at seven thirty.”

“There is a problem though.” She looked at me with that query look of hers that reminded me of Pete. My heart thumped heavily in my chest as I told her as gently as I could who the patient was.

CHAPTER THREE

The Nightmare of Gregory
Hampshire
16 March 1849

I had written the full account of the case that had been thrust upon me, not that I would forget one of the most horrendous cases to date.

Case no. 1391. They charged one FREDERICK BATHO upon the coroner's inquisition only, with feloniously killing and slaying of one Thomas Osborn on 8th July 1848. That ran through my mind every time I closed my eyes.

"And how was it, Detective Sergeant Hampshire...," asked the Defence Lawyer, "... that it took you and your men three days to realise that it was Mr Batho that had killed Mr Osborn?"

"It wasn't three days. We solved that case in three hours, from witness statements of those in the road. It just took us longer to find the guilty party, and I had to start from the beginning after the hash my former colleague had done." I stated firmly.

I relived the nightmare again every time I sleep.

I awakened sweating and gave up sleeping anymore for the night. But last night's nightmare was the worse.

I spoke to Detective Casey Barnston that morning when he remarked on how dreadful I looked. After telling him how I felt, the next day I found myself on the train to Devon.

"And please don't come back until you can close this case in your head." He said at the station. "You did good, lad, but if you burn yourself out like this after every case, then you are no good to me. Got it!?"

"Got it," I said. Knowing the two men were still at large wasn't helping me close the case.

We shook hands, and I climbed aboard the train. I found my seat in a closed compartment and looks like I was on my own. A ticket I had purchased by adding money myself placed me in first class, as I did not want to sit in second class with a lot of strangers. I needed the peace and quiet, but how was I going to clear my mind, and put it into practice, so it never happens again? The answers weren't forthcoming.

I got out my note book and turned to the first page, then closed my eyes and I was back in the courtroom. It was 28th of July, the day of the first court case.

Case 1391. FREDERICK BATHO was charged upon the coroner's inquisition only, with feloniously killing and slaying of one Thomas Osborn.

"How do you plead?"

"Not guilty." Came the stern reply.

I knew then something was wrong. Mr W. J. Payne was conducting the prosecution and called each witness.

William Freeth came to the stand first and gave his statement.

"I live at 6, Galloway-street, St. Luke's. The deceased, Thomas Osborn, lodged in my house and on the 8th of July he came to me at my club, at the Island Queen public-house, about half-past eleven o'clock, and asked for the key. I refused to let him have it, as he was a little the worse for drink, and asked him to come home with me. After a moment's hesitation, he agreed to do so, but only after a few more drinks. We were rather the worse for liquor, and we were sparring about at the Island Queen. We left there a little after one.

When we got outside, Osborn wished to spar with the prisoner, but the prisoner did not want to do anything of the kind. A police officer came up and tried to disperse them, and the prisoner seized Osborn round the arms and body and carried him over the Canal bridge in Wharf Road, telling him to desist. Osborn then accused him of attempting to put his fingers in his pocket and said he would fight any man. The prisoner said he did no such thing. Osborn would fight; the prisoner did not care to do so.

But at last, he said, 'well, if I must fight I must.' So, he gave him one, two, with both hands, and Osborn said, 'that is a nice one; that is a beauty; come on again.'

The police officer laughed with the rest of us.

He had one more hit at him, knocked him backwards, and he fell with the back of his head on the kerb. I helped him up, and the prisoner assisted him part of the way to the police station with me. After we arrived, a police officer said he was arresting us for being drunk. They released us a few hours later. Once home, I left them for a minute and when I came back the prisoner was undoing Osborn's small clothes. I saw him draw his arm back as if putting something into his pocket. I immediately accused him of attempting to rob him.

He replied, 'No such thing.'

I examined Osborn's pockets, and found two pennies, a key, and a small tin pencil case. As I tried to block his getaway, the prisoner made a move on one side, and then ran away through the door, and I saw no more of him. I helped my friend into bed."

The next witness was GEORGE HENRY KIDDELL (*policeman, G* 97).

"I saw the deceased with Freeth and the prisoner leaning against the railing, in Wharf Road. The deceased was bleeding from a minor wound in the back of the head after fighting. I took them to the station and charged them with being drunk and incapable. I placed them in different cells for the night. We discharged them early next morning."

GEORGE MILLER GIBB (*police-inspector, G*).

"They brought the deceased to the station about a quarter past two o'clock on this morning

and he was bleeding from a wound on the head. I sent for Mr. Mather, the police surgeon, and saw him examine his head. He said he thought there was not much to the matter, but the prisoner complained of pain in the head."

MISS MARY TARRANT came next and stated.

"I live at the Three Tons, Horsley Down. I knew the deceased, Thomas Osborn. He was a shoemaker. I live at his father's house as cook and cleaner. He came home on 10th July and asked to see his father, but he collapsed in the hallway. On his father's request, I sent for Mr. Greenwood, a doctor, who attended him until the 19th, when Thomas Osborn died."

HENRY GREENWOOD, Esq. M.D.

"They called me to see the deceased on 10th July. He seemed to have received some serious blow on the head. He was in a semi-comatose state. I found a tiny wound on the back of the head. There was no external evidence of any fracture. I saw him up until that Friday, when he died. I then made a post mortem examination, and I found the occipital bone fractured, or fissured, from the top to the bottom and the anterior lobes of the brain on each side torn. This resulted from a counter-stroke of the blow received from behind. The cause of death was inflammation of the brain, resulting from the injury to the skull. He died with epileptic fits which I attest to and a heavy fall would cause the injuries that I saw."

Prisoner's Defence.*"I am very sorry for the accident that has happened; but according to the witness's statement, I tried all in my power to prevent any fighting. He kept on sparring, shoving, and pushing me about, and would not leave me alone. He insisted on striking me; I did not strike him with any intention of doing him any bodily harm."*

The verdict, to my astonishment, was GUILTY, but strongly recommended to Mercy on account of the provocation he received. He was fined one shilling and discharged.

The next day the man disappeared along with Freeth. Were they in this together? Freeth's testimony bothered me. I ran through it a dozen times.

On 8th July he (Thomas Osborn) came to me at my club, at the Island Queen public-house, about half-past eleven o'clock, and asked for the key. I refused to let him have it.

Key to where, the place where they reside? If so A: why did Thomas Osborn not have one, if he lives there, and B: why was he not given one?

I took these two questions to my boss, who nodded, and he said, "I'll give you one day to look into this. One day mind!"

So, I did. First, Freeth did not own the property of 6, Galloway-Street, St. Luke's, I found out as he stated in court. Therefore, the deceased Thomas Osborn did not lodge in his house. The previous DS had not checked this, nor did he search Osborn's lodgings. The house belonged to a Mrs Jenny Moorhouse, husband deceased. I found out both Freeth and Osborn had lodged there and owed her back rent of almost two shillings each.

I asked to see their rooms. She sniffed. "I let their rooms and sold all their stuff, my right," she said defensively, curling her upper lip and crossing thick arms across an enormous bosom. "But it's not picked up yet. It's in the outhouse, round back." She flicked a finger to the alley at the side of the house.

I went and examined it. Clothes in cheap cases with their names written on the outside, though not more than one extra set as expected. One shirt, one pair of trousers, one scarf, one cardigan, and one coat. Socks that had seen better days for Osborn, yet seemed new for Freeth. There were no trinkets, no mementoes, not even pictures.

But I found something extra in Freeth's things that I did not expect and was the first of three things that bothered me.

First, a purse of ten shillings stitched into the lining of his coat and second, a map folded inside his socks of Brentwood Lunatic Asylum, and thirdly that the landlady had missed both these things. The former two more so than the latter, as I stood there for a little while wondering what they had in common, but by the time I left, I had not fathomed what it was. I took the coat and the socks and told the landlady the rest was hers to do with as she pleased as these were evidence. Smiling, thinking she had the better deal, she closed the door.

I called round to the Dock's office next and spoke to the manager, asking if the two men had worked here as mentioned in the notes of my predecessor, but not mentioned in court. A Mr Teel replied. “Yes, a Thomas Osborn worked here though only a month, and we paid him up to the 7th, never been back since. We employed him as a clerk.” He then asked for the other name again as he went through files. I told him Freeth, William.

“No. No one of that name works here. Now or in the past.”

I thanked him, thinking Freeth's story was definitely full of holes. But why hadn’t Detective Sargent Henry Barfield checked it. He was an experienced DS, or so I was told, but then resigned from the police force. Unusual, but not unheard of and no one had seen him since.

Had Osborn gone for a drink and Freeth found him and tried to rob him? Was the ten Bob Osborn's? Ten shillings was a lot, but how did it get sewn into Freeth's coat? I still had one more place to visit, hoping to shed some light on the case. My feet hurried across town.

I called around to the Three Tons, on Horsley Down. A strange name for a house of some means, by the look of it. Osborn was or would have been a man of property. Therefore, the ten Bob could have been his.

His father was a retired shoemaker and said his son kept no keys to his lodgings there. Osborn’s father explained his son would have taken over the family business, but they argued, and he declined to take it on. Osborn would rather be a dock working clerk. He was an only child, as his mother had died in childbirth. Over this last year, he’d seen him only a few times and did not understand why he did not want to take on the business. He was apparently a fine craftsman and had a good head for figures. The father had never met his friends and the names, Freeth or Batho rang no bells. I thanked him and took my leave.

My next call was to the Manhattan club, upstairs, at the Island Queen public house on Queen's Street, and I got a frosty reception from the barmen.

"No one called Freeth is a member here, nor anyone called Batho."

The tall dark-haired man was clearly lying, as he would not look me in the eye as he answered, but alone, with no backup, I left the smarmy git to his drying glasses.

Back at the station, I looked in at the library room and asked the desk sergeant about Brentwood Asylum as I have not yet fathomed that one out. They have not built it yet, I was informed, still in the foundation stage. Now I was even more confused.

What, therefore, had the place to do with two crooks? I knew they were doing a number on Osborn. I suspected it in the courthouse, but just did not know what? But I was sure that's what Freeth and Batho were as I made my way upstairs to the CID office.

There, I spoke to the boss. First, I told what I had done all day. Then said, but with little satisfaction. "What do you make of this?"

"Hmm," he replied, fingering the socks. "These are new, excellent quality too." Then he smiled as he withdrew the contents. After looking at the unfolded paper, he added. “Brentwood, it’s new, isn’t it?” As he saw the internal drawing of Brentwood Lunatics Asylum, “Not yet built.”

I nodded. I handed him the coat next, and once he found the purse, he threw the coat in the bin.

“But what’s the connection to the ten shillings and why didn’t he come back to claim it?” I watched as he put the shillings in a drawer.

“Good questions, so what’s next?” He looked straight at me.

I looked at him, startled. He’s the boss, and he tells me what to do. “I have no idea.” I stated dumbly.

“Tut, tut boy. Come on, that's not good enough. You picked up something from the courthouse, now you’ve picked up something from 6 Galloway Street, and you’ve deemed they were doing a number on Osborn, so where too next?”

I looked at his desk and saw the map, and said hesitantly “Brentwood?”

“Well done, save all expense receipts, but don’t go mad. We’re not made of money. Be back on Thursday night and back at work on Friday. Okay?”

I nodded. To my astonishment he gave me five shillings from his locked drawer and told me to write up the reports and I was to call if I find anything that takes me further afield or needed a bigger name to the locals. And he would have a letter of introduction later.

“Okay.” I nodded again. I went back to my desk and began writing up all I needed. I even went down to the information office and asked more questions. At six, I left for the night.

Early the next morning, I boarded the train to Colchester with my overnight bag and my note case. I would alight in Brentford at 08:40 in just over half an hour. While I travelled, I read the two reports I had brought with me, as well as my own.

One report said: 1844 report, new asylums sprouted up across the country for the crazies as they dubbed them as there was a rising tide of mental illness, but had no inmates as yet, so those were not included, one of which was Brentwood. It listed all asylums apart from workhouses.

Below there were a lot of addresses, I noted, but some workhouses have lunatic wards. This was because the Inquiry Commission did not systematically visit workhouses as it did with other asylums. This was because most asylums would only take certain cases. Picky, I thought. The report continued for another four pages, but I put it aside as it did not help. I wondered what the site of an asylum and two crooks had in common? I came up with a big fat zero!

Tired of useless thinking, I picked up the other report and read. They identified the site within the Brentwood Hall Estate for the construction of an asylum. Kendall & Pope designed the asylum in the High Victorian Gothic style to a corridor plan layout, much like Hanley, near where I live. The foundation stone wouldn't be laid until October 1851 and named as the Essex County Lunatic Asylum and they would not officially open the hospital until September 1853. Neither were complete enough to operate any staff, including security.

So, not in use yet. Therefore, just a building site, so what was so important about it? Nothing there helped either, but I noted a few things in my notebook. So many questions and not enough answers. The half hour passed quickly and soon the train was pulling into Brentwood Station, so I cleared my things back into my note case. I reached for my overnight bag and made my way to the door. Although, I still could not fathom what this was all about as I exited the train.

Chief Inspector Mayfield, a tall yet lean man compared to my chief, met me. This chief was bright and missed little. As we walked through the town, he listened to a quick resume of events from London and then later, once in his office, he read the reports that I'd brought with me. Including a letter from my Chief Inspector, that was addressed personally to him, which thankfully he did not dismiss out of hand. I knew of clashes with neighbouring county police officers. Though my Chief Inspector out-ranked him by a few extra medals, mine did not make that apparent in his letter and asked if he could help his junior officer with any information in ascertaining if these criminals were there on his patch. Then it gave a brief outline, not only of the disappearances of the two men wanted now in questioning of murder and suspected robbery, but apparently attested to my character of putting to bed nasty cases like this one.

Hence my reason for joining the CID local office.

"Fine work, Sergeant," he praised, looking up.

"Let's see if we cannot only add to this but finish it too and we can both add it to our resumes." His smile seemed genuine.

That night, with a half a dozen men, we headed to the Brentwood Lunatic Asylum. We arrived at the north entrance and found the gate unbolted and the chain laying on the ground; the gates wide open. The chief nodded to me before waiving us through.

We entered the grounds as quietly as possible and separating as the dirt road came to a junction. Some hurried around to the back. We hurried up to the foundations of what looked to be an extensive building in the making. There were many workmen's buildings that, once they finished the work, they would take them down or move them as the building progressed but were placed just in the right position for looking as we narrowed the search parameter to the main building.

It wasn't long to establish that there were four men digging a hole that had no business upon these grounds. Well, technically two were digging, the other two were watching. As we watched, the two diggers must have made the hole big enough to state, there was 'nought here,' and scrambled out of it. What we did not expect was one to say 'now' as another walked behind one digger and astonishingly, slit his throat. That was enough for the local chief, and soon the local force surrounded the three men and took them into custody as the fourth bled out at their feet. I was in their territory, so could only watch.

"Apparently, a falling out of thieves," stated the Chief Inspector, yet there was more to this I was certain. I had enough; let someone else find out why they were digging a hole in the grounds of a not yet built, asylum in Brentwood. They were not the men I was looking for, and I had enough on my plate.

While two men waited for the coroner's carriage for the now dead man, they marched the others off towards Coptford Road police station, there after a little persuading, we found out they had been staying at the crown and had searched three rooms. Oddly enough, we found an ornamental box. Not knowing what it was for, I took it with me to find out, as London had more resources than Brentwood.

I went back to the station where I was questioned and left my statement with the duty sergeant, leaving out my suspicions. I promised to return on the date of the hearing for a charge of trespassing and murder upon the three men.

The chief was sure the box was old, so they must have stolen it. I, at that time, could not argue. As these weren't the ones I was after, but the three men knew Freeth and Batho, I was sure as each reacted to the names when given, though in different ways. Two looked scared, and the other sneered.

I picked up my bags from the duty sergeant and negated an overnight stay; I left and was back on the train before midnight, going home. I'd sleep all tomorrow before being back to the station on Friday. That was a week ago.

By 8th October, I was still not sleeping, and I went through this case again. I was back in Brentwood and gave evidence against the three men. While there, one stated they were doing what they were told by a man named Grimshaw. He paid them two shillings each to find another box like the one I had removed back to London with me, buried in the grounds of the looney bin as he called the Asylum. The man killed had opened his gob, I was told, and they shut it for him, permanently as ordered. The box was this Grimshaw's, who was Army and Brentwood was the wrong place. Now what did that mean? I wondered.

The box looked like an antique, but I found nothing else about it even in London's low markets.

I spoke to a Captain Charles Blakeman of Orange Street recruitment office later that Friday and I said, "I'm making enquiries concerning a man named Grimshaw."

"That would be Captain Oliver Grimshaw, Green Howard, Richmond Barracks North Yorkshire, but the captain was out of the country attending to her Majesty's affairs."

I deduced that meant either India or Sri Lanka as both had been in the papers recently, and I would get nothing more, so that was a bust. I left.

By late November, I had got nowhere near to the bottom of this case. I could not trace Grimshaw through police informers. As this was now a cold case, I had other duties. I did not pick it up again till late February when Bow Street picked up a man named Batho for drunk and disorderly. They left the information on my desk on a freezing, late Friday morning.

I hurried round there, only to find out they had released the man, not more than an hour before, frustration hit like a hammer, but I could check the file for details. As if that helped. An address given was 10 Queens Street; the Manhattan Club. So, Batho and Freeth knew each other.

I took a stroll, trying to keep warm. I lingered on the corner and watched the premises, stamping my feet to keep the cold out of my leather shoes. The building was on three streets; Greek Street ran down one side, Hog Street ran along to an alley way at the back, and Queens Street went across the top. The lower half of the building was the Queens Head public house, with the board of her Majesty's head including crown hung off a metal rod between the first-floor windows, belonging to the Manhattan club.

There was a side door on Greek Street which few used. By lunch time, the main doors of the pub, saw a lot of opening and closing, but my guess, it was the side door I needed to monitor. But I had been here too long, and I ought to report in to the Station and a sandwich would not go amiss.

Sadly, I turned only to see Batho himself on the opposite side of the road, hurrying towards the Queens. My gander was up, but I could not take him on alone. I turned, so he did not see me, and then watched him disappear in through the side door. I almost ran back to the Station.

Within an hour, we had gathered five men and moved in. I stood on the corner and watched from the opposite street.

We had to wait for a bow street runner to bring the warrants, so we could arrest him and Freeth, if he was within as well. Anticipation and eagerness flushed through my system, competing with each other as I stamped my feet in the afternoon sunshine, that brought no warmth.

Twenty minutes after arriving, Batho re-appeared just as a black cab pulled up and before we could react, Batho jumped in the cab and the horse cantered off down the road, away from us. One officer ran after it, but the rest of us stood around waiting. There was no movement around the public house.

Thirty minutes, to the Chief's annoyance, the warrants arrived, and we went in. By the time we had climbed the stairs, his temper had not improved. It was empty except for a barman.

"Sorry Gents," the smarmy guy replied, "no one fitting that description has been here. Members only here, check the pub downstairs, they apparently let anyone in."

Suddenly, without warning, the chief's right arm flew across the bar and grabbed the guy by his shirt, pulling him bodily down to the bar. "Now, sweetheart, do you want to run that by me again?"

"I tell yer, I don't know these guys."

"Funny," said the chief inspector, "Batho left here only an hour ago and stayed twenty minutes."

"What, big guy, cleft chin? He ain't no member, he delivered a letter for a member, that's all."

"Who?" prompted the Chief, pushing down the man's face further to the wood, distorting his face.

"Grimshaw, Captain Grimshaw." Came the muffled reply.

"Give," said the chief, releasing the man, who

reached underneath the bar. “Careful, sunshine, you don’t want an attempted murder charge being applied to your corpse.” Said the chief with a nasty grin as he showed him his own weapon that I did not know he carried.

Shocked, then looked as if butter didn't melt. “Here.” He pulled a white folded sheet of paper sealed with plain candle wax out from under the bar.

The chief moved away from the bar as he broke the seal. “Let’s see who’s contacting a captain of her Majesty's armed forces.” He paused as he unfolded the paper.

O. I saw over his shoulder. ***Everything’s going according to plan, we should have a new master by the end of February. Brentwood wasn’t a total bust and the two obstacles won’t be a problem much longer either. Come round when you get back. D.***

“Need to talk,” I mumbled.

He nodded. He refolded the paper, using its own creases and tipped some wax from the candle lamp from the nearby table back on the paper to reseal it. Then he handed it back to the barman. “You’ve got a choice. Either tell Grimshaw that I know or tell me when Grimshaw collects his mail. I’m the better deal. Got it?!” The barman nodded.

Back outside I told him I knew the Brentwood Saga wasn’t over and I need to go back and warn their CI. They deserved to be warned.

“Agreed, but I’ll send a letter.” Replied the boss.

The nightmare was getting worse and still

rattled around my brain and I was losing sleep over it.

"And how was it, Detective Sergeant Hampshire, that it took you and your men three days to realise that it was Mr Batho that had killed Mr Osborn?" asked the prosecution, who turned his distorted face to mine. I flinched.

"It wasn't three days, your honour." I spoke as calmly as I could looking at the judge, yet seethed inside, but my resolve was melting fast. "We solved that case in three hours, from witness statements of those in the road at the time, but we did not let the two responsible go, the court did."

"But you let him kill again in those three hours, did you not, Detective Sergeant?" The prosecutor stated. His face turned again, looking like the gargoyle in Saint Thomas's church.

Fear gripped my insides.

"No! No, he did not." I tossed and turned before I awoke, sweating. This had to stop!

Now, I'm on a couple of days R and R, resting till Friday as ordered. On Monday, I will attend my friend's funeral, or I hope to. Things had a habit of changing in my life so fast I barely had time to sit down, and I still had not caught Freeth and Batho. Had they even been in Brentwood? Was Brentwood even the place? Could Brentwood be a person? This worried me, as I had friends who were 'Brentwood' and they had just lost a son to strange circumstances. How was I going to put all I had learned into practice?

I picked up my note book and turned to the first page, then closed my eyes. It was 28th of July, the day of the court case. What was this trying to tell me? What had I missed? I sat outside in the hallway but could hear every word as I waited my turn to give evidence, but nothing changed. Restless I went for a walk, but I still could not put it together as I went around my family's estate in Devon and even after two days R and R, I had got no further. Two men ripped off a third, possibly on this Captain Grimshaw's orders. Four men in Brentwood looking for a box similar to the one I'm looking for or belonging to the very same Captain.

I was back in London on Saturday and on Sunday, the chief called me into the office.

On the 18th of March a note appeared on the chief's desk saying 'Sweetheart,' miss my 'sunshine.' Please come and see me at 8, had arrived.

It took a moment to work out who 'sweetheart and sunshine' were and for the chief to stop laughing.

We strolled around to the Queen's pub and entered by the side door at 07:45. The chief was in two minds whether it was a setup. This time the place wasn't empty. Even the lights were dimmed, so it was difficult to find out just how many were in the place. An icy shiver ran up my spine. I chose a table by the door as was told and the chief went to the bar. The rest, two other CID officers and constables had waited downstairs in case the two were here and did a runner. The chief thought I could call them when needed. I was thinking the chief was right.

I watched closely, keeping the chief in view at

all times. Even when asked by the pretty girl, 'what do you want to drink?'

"Bourbon," I replied, "on the rocks." I added as I laid a sixpence on her tray and waited only to notice the Chief hadn't moved. The drink arrived, but it went untouched as fear rose within me as I saw two men at the bar inch closer to the boss. A chill now froze the fear within me.

I got to my feet to go to him, when I was joined by a large man, Batho! Though where he had come from, I did not know. My blood was now artic as he put his hand on my shoulder and held me down. At first, I tried to wriggle free, but to no avail. I watched, powerless, as three more large heavies walked to the chief. My Chief turned and knew as I did things looked in their favour, but he did not have time to pull out his gun as one thumped him on the chin. The chief took it and though for a few moments he gave as good as he got and got to punch back the first guy, others caught his arms and then they all laid into him. The barman smiled maliciously as I tried to call out, but the door was now closed. Then I tried again to move to go to the chief's aid, though a quarter of his size, but Batho's hand kept me down. Fear they may have killed him grew within as the chief went down.

Then Batho let go quickly. I did not expect what came next, he clobbered me. I hit the table hard knocking the whiskey over before I blacked out.

CHAPTER FOUR

Miss Samantha Danvers
7th March 1849

Dear Diary,

The night of a ten thousand lights ball fast approaches. I cannot wait!

The Debutants Ball. The overall spirit of this era's dancing in 1849 was one of excitement, exuberance and gracious romance. Romance my foot, even though the dances were fresh, inventive, youthful and somewhat daring as the papers put it. Society fashions are rich, elegant, and costly, but continued an emphasis on simplicity, yet I knew what my cousin would say. It served a purpose, the only purpose, the Marriage Markets. I hated it and I was part of it, just like she was, I thought this afternoon as I rode through Hyde Park showing myself off. Miss Samantha Danvers, Debutant, ready for marriage at my father's discretion.

"Soon, the Major Event will take place and the eligible and not so eligible will knock on my door," said my father assuredly, "and you had best pick the right one!"

Yes, the one you want! It rankled that I had no choice. I had walked out of his office as sedately as I could, though tears were streaming down my face, by the time I got to my room. Luckily, no one saw as I ran to my bed after I had closed my door as softly as I could. I did not want another lecture on closing doors in his house. I slept badly that night too afraid to dream of Steven.

I reported downstairs at seven-thirty exactly the next morning. There were no extra hours to dally in this house, I was told when I was five. My day starts at seven every morning. It was lessons until five on how to behave, to sit, to stand when to laugh, to play the piano, cards, and dance. What subjects I could speak on and then two hours on the classics before retiring at ten with a quiz to make sure I had read to the very last word. Meals were at seven-thirty, one, and seven-thirty sharp. Though I felt far from eating this morning as I could get. I kissed my mother's cheek and was thankful my father had gone to his office in the city. I was apprehensive what came next. Not one morning since I reached seventeen had I had a moment's peace.

"Have you sorted your dress for Saturday?" My mother stated as I picked up my fork.

Anyone would think you want rid of me. I thought as I ate slowly and chewed thoughtfully, waiting for the lecture.

"Well, you have been a troublesome child, to say the least, Samantha, and frankly, your father and I have had enough. Young ladies don't ask questions all the time, they learn things that will be useful in their married life to amuse their husbands. Their role in life is to keep their fathers happy, then their husbands, bring children into this world that can help the husband financially, not drain it. You certainly have drained it."

I wondered, *how?*

"How," she continued without pausing, "many young ladies do you know have five ball gowns, twenty-five-day dresses and five riding habits, eh? I'll tell you," She continued without pausing again, "None. That's how many. None! So, you will ride every morning, entertain every afternoon and go to five balls this season until someone with money and a title asks for your hand. And if you dare deviate from that, I'll lock you up in Hanley as the disobedient girl you are and don't think for one moment I won't. I think you've eaten enough. Now go out and ride till noon. I don't want to see you before then and don't go anywhere but the park. Do you understand?"

I got up, walked sedately to her chair and said, "Yes, mama." I kissed her dutifully and left and all the time, I was thinking, I'll find the meanest man I can. One who will give you all the help you deserve and more and takes you for every single penny and assets you have got. And with that in mind and a grim smile on my face, I ran lightly up the stairs to get ready to look for my rich, horrible husband.

Though the face of Steven clouded my brain.

The ride into the park had been uneventful, and Moneyash walked behind me at a sedate pace. I felt like kicking the horse and galloping off into the sunshine, just to make him run. But knowing my father, he would find me and drag me back by my hair for a good spanking and one of those was bad enough.

Just then, I saw Catherine come from the other end and my heart rejoiced. I had not seen her in over six months. She stopped the carriage beside my horse.

"Samantha, how fortunate," she said, removing herself from her seat and came towards me.

I thought quickly, *could she help?*

"Catherine," I acknowledged. "Forgive my tardiness and my condolences for your brother." She nodded and gave a slightly tight smile. I saw the sadness in her eyes, and my guilt deepened.

"Will you join us next Sunday and go with the family on Monday?" she asked. We had grown close over the years and mother had sent me to learn how to be a lady from my cousin and she had taught me many things I have never disclosed to my parents.

I would be there, I told her, in my assuredness that my parents would let me go. Peter was my cousin after all. Well, technically, I was his third cousin. My mother was second, but she rarely spoke to Mabel Brentwood. My mother thinks that her husband is far superior to Lord Brentwood. I would give anything to have been born a Brentwood, not a Danvers. I had always felt welcomed in the

Brentwood's home, more so than in my own.

Leaning down, I whispered. "Talk to me Sunday, I need your help." Then straightened up as Moneyash was coming forward. I saw the puzzled look in her eyes, but a swift look to the footman, and it cleared. She nodded her understanding.

"I'll see you next week, please take care and again my condolence."

She nodded and another smile. We parted, and I rode on after a quick look at Moneyash.

That night my father came to my room, and I quickly hid my diary. He was thundering mad. "You had no business talking to the Brentwood girl, and I don't give a damn about her brother. The lot will die if I had my way." He raged on for ten minutes on how much better he was than Peter Brentwood Senior, or that old general Johnson, he was after all the queen's under minister for overseas affairs. What were they? Country doctors no more. He continued to rant while I cowered in the corner.

Peter Brentwood was the leader of the medical board and attends the Queen. I was sure Catherine had told me a long time ago. Then my father left, slamming the door. I put my diary in the bottom of my bag and slept sitting up, too afraid to sleep. The rest of the week passed and nothing changed, but the weather.

14th March 1849

Dear Diary,

Sunday came, and I got ready to leave as I

thought my parents found no objection to my attendance at the funeral so far and had not said I could not go, nor a night away from home. My father, it seemed, had relented.

I went down to the stable after lunch to see if the carriage was ready, but found it unmanned and still in the coach house. Strange. I stepped around to the right-hand side of the brougham to see if Moneyash was inside the opened doors. It was too dark to see too far inside, so I stepped to the carriage. I then stepped inside and while I waited, I added a line or two to my diary. I was about to put it away in my overnight bag as I saw Moneyash was heading this way from the house, though I did not like the look on his face.

CHAPTER FIVE

Finding Oliver Grimshaw
Tuesday, 16th March 1849

John Beckett
Orange Street Barracks

The St George was a military installation on Orange Street in Westminster and was the main recruiting depot for the London area.

Corporal Etterwood and I dressed and walked like any other soldier in the barracks and made our way to the Officer's mess without being accosted. They had stopped us at the main gate and asked about our business.

To which I said, "I am Captain Beckett and was here to attend upon Captain Charles Blakeman on family business," and the gate opened.

Captain Blakeman was a career man at orange street. He ran the records office for recruiting office and was an old friend.

Charles greeted me at the door and brought us inside. He offered both of us seats. I introduced the Corporal. They shook hands.

"You're here about Peter, aren't you?" The man held my look as I gave a nod.

"Not right, they informed top brass about his death, but the colonel here said something fishy was going on there in Sri-Lanka, in more ways than one, make no mistake. So, what can I do for you?"

"Tell me of a recruit named Oliver Grimshaw, rank Captain. Green Howards, Yorkshire Regiment."

Charles flipped a switch and told his batman to find the file. "And now." He added. Then he asked after the father. "How's old Peter, this can't be easy and not doing him any good?"

"He managed the funeral yesterday but took to his bed after we got back. The daughters are taking care of him with their mother. The surviving son, James, is studying to be a doctor and divides his time between his work and home, but the Corporal here is an adopted Brentwood and is helping. Pete's death has hit them all hard especially, as it was murder."

"Yes, heard of many tales on and off the battlefield, but that one was horrendous to say the least." There was a knock at the door.

"File you asked for, sir." A tall thin man stepped into the office wearing glasses.

"Thanks, Mansfield. I'll call you if I need anything else."

The door closed before Charles opened the file. "This bothers me, as the police called here about the same man, a few months ago. Now then let's see." He picked up the one sheet and wave it in the air. "Strange, every file is about an inch thick unless you are a raw recruit. This is unbelievable." He pressed the switch again on the intercom and spoke to Mansfield.

"All there was Captain and no file release." Then there was a pause. "Remember that break in last week, but they took nothing, unless…" He paused again.

Charles muttered. "Check all files and let me know if there is any more and who?"

"Yes Captain." The intercom clicked off.

Charles frowned. "Never understood the break-in. Did not know what there was that could be stolen, but we captured the man trying to break in, so end of case. But now, was he trying to reseal the door after he had got in and out and we got it wrong, yet he had nothing on him?"

I glanced at Steven as Charles looked down. "A partner," I stated.

"Possible," replied the other Captain as he turned back to the sheet in hand. "Oliver Johnson Grimshaw. Parents: the late Colin Grimshaw and Maureen Johnson Grimshaw of Blanesfield, North Yorkshire. Born 1821 in Blanesfield. Moved to India 1825, Returned 1834. Enlisted, not recruited, 1846, age 25. Green Howards, North Yorkshire Regiment. Bought his way in. Captainship was questioned by one Colonel Harry Danvers, also of the Green Howards'. He judged him capable, and they sent him to India in 1846 with the relief, then on to Ceylon in 1848. He returned to Richmond

Barracks 7th March 1849. Says here he was training to be a boot smith at his father's factory in 1834, but after his father's death, they sold the factory as a going concern and the family left. Nothing more until he enlisted, as I said in '46."

"Where is he now?" I asked.

"Yorkshire, I presume as all relief are now back in the country. He's something to do with Sargent Brentwood's death I presume?"

I nodded. I explained he was mentioned in Pete's Journal. There was nothing more on the sheet, so we took our leave. We hurried back to the house. Catherine was waiting in the hall, clearly agitated. I had barely time to remove my coat as she took ahold of my hand and pulled me into the sitting room. Steven followed, and the others were waiting.

"Do you remember this from my brother's journal?" She asked before I had sat down. "But they got this sergeant's attention." She continued as I nodded. "'Treasure, Ruin, and Brentwood. I was sure, they weren't talking about me.' How was he so sure?" she asked. I shook my head; I had no idea. She continued "'A lot?" asked Grimshaw. "Yes," replied the other.' A lot of what, treasure? I agreed with this because you said yourself there was no treasure, but people kept looking?"

I nodded. She continued. "'No, the journal goes on, it's absolutely true. Belongs to Thomas Becket, Archbishop of Canterbury, no less. But if you breathe a word of this, it will find us in a ditch with no voice boxes, okay?'" She looked at me, causing my heart to flutter. "Was this blond waving a pot of gold under Grimshaw's nose or was it under my brother's?" She paused for a moment and when she looked at me, my heart lurched. This clearly upset her, and she was trying hard not to show it.

"What happens if you look at this a different way? Try, Treasure, Ruin and Brentwood. The three words heard and noted by my brother. Treasure in the ruins at Brentwood. That's what my brother and all of us thought, but another way, a scary way. Destroy their treasure to ruin the Brentwood's or to bring about their ruin. What can ruin a family's good name?" She asked me. Her lips trembled.

"A scandal." I replied softly.

"What treasures does this family have, that could fit in this scenario?" She asks.

I shook my head, not knowing Sir Peter Brentwood's finances or assets.

She supplied the answer. "My father's children. My father always said, we are his greatest treasures and assets. How can they ruin us, that could cause a scandal?" Her eye's wide with anxiety and fear.

"Entrapment into marriage, by kidnapping." I hissed. My chest muscles tightened.

She nodded again. "So, what they said in that tent may have another meaning, because they knew he was listening. But forewarned is forearmed as they say, look what I found in the back of his journal?"

I read the words that acted like a drum in my heart. What was this Grimshaw up to?

Follow Grimshaw to see where he leads.

Captain: Either Green Howard or 2nd Madras Regiment? Can he be both?

EIC: East India Company, trades in Cotton, silks, indigo dye, salt, spices, saltwater, tea, coffee, and opium, not to mention human trafficking. Does he work for or against the EIC?

Patrick Van's Agnew and Lieutenant William Anderson. Killed 1842 who and why? Anglo Sikh war began because of their deaths. Patrick was a civil servant, yet was a leader of EIC? Did he know Grimshaw? Were they killed because of his membership to EIC?

What Connection to cousin Harry Danvers? To Samantha Danvers? To Gillian Turner? To Gracie Fletcher?

1 Greek Street/ Hogs Lane, called Manhattan Club, in and out twice a week in '45. Was he a member? Unknown. What is this club to Grimshaw? Unknown.

History 1811, no longer residential and let to Westminster commissioners of sewers. Maps of underground sewers are supposed to be kept there? There's a Chapel close by and a public house called Queens below the club. Significance to either? Unknown as yet. Where do the sewers run to?

Catherine waited until I looked up. "I found this on the last page and thought it was better here?" I handed it to Steven, who, after reading it, passed it on. I watched their faces as each read it before Catherine added. "What if my brother wasn't working alone?"

Now they all had distinct looks.

“A spy.” I said, with a puzzled look.

“Certainly not!” said Andy firmly, yet with a look that said, he was not sure. The same for Steven. But Davis’ was the best.

“Spill?” she said, looking at him. I and the others looked his way too, but just that moment James arrived and entered in a rush.

“Catherine, your assistance please.” He turned before she could object. This was important, but resignedly she went.

I followed, puzzled. I went out of the door with the others following. In the hall stood two other gentlemen and a young woman, who I later found out was their second cousin, Samantha Danvers.

“Catherine?” she called, reaching out. Catherine pulled her into an embrace, as the situation clearly confused and frightened the woman.

“I’m sorry Catherine, but things are different, but for now, a bed and plenty of rest, please sister.” James asked of Catherine.

“Take her upstairs. Steven, be good enough to help cousin Samantha upstairs, please.”

Steven propelled Samantha gently to the stairs. She clutched tightly to his hand. Catherine followed, but turned when she heard her brother turn to the others. “If you’ll all step back into the room. I need a drink before I explain.” I followed them inside and the door closed.

CHAPTER SIX

A Harrowing Tale
23 March 1849

Catherine Brentwood, Writing in Peter Brentwood's Journal

"Samantha," I inquired, once upstairs, "are you alright?"

"Sure, Catherine, a bang on the head, that's all. Can't remember anything before waking up at that place. Can't remember leaving home and arriving here yesterday or falling either. Though to be sure." She moved to the bed, a little wobbly on her legs. "Do you mind, I feel exhausted?"

I looked at Steven as he stood in the door of the only free guest bedroom left and I mouthed the word, 'what?' He shrugged. I waved him away as I shut the door, though no sooner had I got back to the bed, a knock came. "Hello," I called, as I had already reached out to help undress her.

"It's me, Peggy, Miss, came to help." Came the reply.

"Come in, Peggy. Fetch a nightdress from my room, please." The door opened and closed again, and a few minutes elapsed when it did it again, bringing Peggy back. Within moments, Samantha was in bed and resting. Apparently, James had told Peggy that it has been over twenty-four hours since the fall. Therefore, Miss Samantha can sleep.

I left Peggy watching over my cousin and told her to call me if she needed me. Then I went quietly, though thoughtfully, downstairs. I hurried to the sitting room and entered.

"How is she?" asked James, standing up after putting down the whisky tumbler.

"Falling asleep," I replied. "What's going on? Why does she think she was here and fell?"

"That would be me." I turned to see a foreign gentleman, who had also got to his feet. Tall, black-haired, Indian possibly. "I have taken away her memory for now and supplied her with one she can cope with. She was catatonic when Doctor Harfield called me in this afternoon. Something had terrified her to such a state, she closed down."

"Not convention, I assure you. This is Raptu Singh, a hypnotist." Put in the other unfamiliar face. Doctor Harfield, I presumed.

I nodded my head to each as they said their names. "But, do you know how she got this way?" I asked.

Doctor Harfield shook his head. "All I know is that when I returned after lunch four days ago, I found my top orderly had put her in room two. I sent a message to the address that the man had given calling himself her husband. And there was no response. So, I sent Collins out to find out. In fact, the address was a school."

"She has no husband," I replied. "I called around to her home address yesterday but found no one home. Does it give a name?"

"O. Grimms." Was the reply.

I looked at John. "You don't think Oliver Grimshaw?"

He shrugged. "Anything is possible."

"But we know there is a connection, Peter wrote it in his journal." I added.

"Yes, and seems cousin Harry is Colonel Harry Danvers, who signed off on Grimshaw's Captaincy."

"You're joking?" James sat down heavily. "I was going to wait till tomorrow after you and I had seen her, but when I read her file, I needed to ask a few personal questions, so I went back to see Doctor Harfield. They took me to see her after assurances that nothing untoward had happened to her, but we all kept our distance. Yet as though she felt my presence, she suddenly looked in my direction and ran into my arms, sobbing hysterically and would not let me go. 'He tried to kill me!' She blurted. 'I did not know him.' Which she stated repeatedly. Then Raptu Singh arrived. A hypnotist, I was told, and once she was under hypnosis, the story came out. We also found her diary, and it tells a different picture of the one they led us to believe, especially from her parents. She's been a virtual prisoner while they waited for her to grow up and ready to find a husband worthy of her parents, except for her training, including it seems even you, Catherine. What happened after her marriage, they did not care as long as she brought the wealth and prestige they required."

Steven had gone a pale colour and reached for the whisky. I knew he had feelings for her from the few times she would visit.

I looked at my brother's journal and saw the page with the list of names. Then looked at my brother, James. I had shown him the list. He already knew about the book from the night before last as we talked about showing it to our friends.

James explained to the group what he knew. "Grimms, Captain in two different regiments. Possible, he worked for the East India Company as the Madras Army was working for them too, plus he grew up in both India and travelled with his father until the father died. He was a wealthy man in shoe factories in both places here and abroad. The EIC were nothing more than pirates and is known at the palace. Slaves, opium and that's just two, they are into anything that's illegal," James added. "Information trading mostly and Lord above, who knows what else. Father kept me abreast of the politics of the palace. Is Danvers mixed up with EIC?"

I shook my head, and I took up the theorizing. "Pete also puts a question mark besides Samantha's name and a few others and there's two other girls, named Gillian Turner and Gracie Fletcher as well and there's a mention of two men that were killed in 1842. Patrick Van's Agnew and Lieutenant William

Anderson, but not why someone killed them? Unless because they worked for EIC. But what's the connection to this Grimshaw? And, finally there is a house connected to Grimshaw, or at least a club called the Manhattan. Its address is 1 Greek Street on the corner of Queen's Street. Now if the O. Grimms is Oliver Grimshaw, that means he was away from Barracks at least a week ago, with or without a good reason. And responsible for Samantha's kidnapping. So, what are each of you doing tomorrow, while I stay and look after my cousin? Maybe an official letter penned from you, James, in our father's name, telling Uncle Danvers that Samantha is here and after a slight fall is recovering, though I would like to see his face as he reads it. But be careful how you word it, especially if he is part of the EIC." He nodded. "John," she continued turning to him with a smile, "what are you doing? "

"Steven and I are off on a train tomorrow. No, hold that thought, I'll send a telegram to the Colonel at the Barracks in Yorkshire and see if Grimshaw is there first, and while I'm waiting maybe accompany James. I think a visit is better than a letter. I too would like to meet your cousin. Maybe, Steven, you could keep an eye on here after you visit the local police station and find the one who called at Orange Street?" Steven nodded.

"Maybe you can speak to my brother, if he's there?" put in Mags.

"Good idea, on all accounts," I said. "Now Davis, don't think for one moment I had forgotten you. Spill?"

"Secret service!" He stunned us all. I sat down; this was too much!

"What? Never!" stated Andy. "Surely not."

"Aye, they caught him at school, I guess. Always has to dig a little deeper, did our Peter, always making side notes, that's our Peter, got himself noticed, got himself killed!" He finished angrily, slapping a fist on a table, making us all jump.

The room hushed.

What had my brother got himself into? I thought unhappily. I looked up and caught John's eye. A look of concern bathed over his face. I smiled, hoping to ease that feeling.

"Noooo, I don't believe it!" said Andy softly, finally breaking the silence.

"Okay," said John, "a spy needs a handler so, who's his?"

"Can't help I'm afraid, I only guessed that, but it fits especially with that last page." Commented Davis.

"Emlyn Jonstone," replied James, "though don't quote me. Saw Pete talking to him once. He works for the Department for Sewers Commissioners, but whether it's another name for EIC? You got me on that one! Yet he's not been seen since Christmas, his office was in Whitehall and the next day, he was talking to Greg's boss and as Peter had never been in trouble, I thought it was weird then and still think that today. Two days later, Pete was off to Orange Street."

"Aye, he told me," Put in Andy, "that a change of scenery would do him good."

"Gregory Hampshire knows about my brother's secret service activities?"

"He never said a word to me," put in Mags crossly.

"Hmm, I'm thinking more military intelligence," put in John.

"Yes, I too have to go along with that," said Davis. "Stands to reason, why join the army and why send him there to India. After all, East India Company has an army of its own, doesn't need ours, unless he was to watch over them, but at what cost? Besides, the Secret Service has no jurisdiction, it would be a military one."

"Grandpa?!" said both James and I together.

"He would have been behind this I'm sure, but he died, and who took over? And why would Jonstone be talking to Peter if they are a front for EIC? Besides," I added, "several saw Grimshaw going into the offices of the Sewers Commission regularly on Greek Street, which we now know is the Manhattan club. Unless he was to see someone, as Peter wouldn't be working for them and it would give a reason why he wanted to enlist the year after leaving college rather than doing the usual European jaunt, like everyone else. Was it because he was told to follow Grimshaw, who had enlisted two months before?"

"Besides, the government is looking into the practices of the East India Company." They looked at me as though I had grown two heads or something. "What a girl can't read the Daily Standard. Father leaves it lying around, so, I borrow it. Sandalwood soap shares are up ten shillings, so father will make a fortune when he sells."

James shook his head as he said with a worried frown. "Father has no shares in Daniel's company."

"Yes, he does. My allowance was worth losing for a month and father's broker had no reason to suspect it wasn't father's money or his note. Daniel needed our backing as a member of our family. As I deal with all father's correspondence now, I helped, and he's a member of the board, which will be down to you. Besides, the point is, I know a lot more than I should and there's a lot I'd like to replace. So, what else do I need to know?"

"The two other women whose names are with Samantha's?" Mags reminded me.

"Yes, Davis, Andy, go see if they are on the high born or low born register and an address if you can. I have a feeling I know these; I just cannot place them." Both heads nod.

"Hadn't thought of that," put in Davis.

"James, as you're with John and are going to see Uncle Harry's reaction when you tell him about Samantha, I am curious how she got there? Did you bring the admissions sheet with you, sir?" I turned to the Doctor as James and John nodded. Doctor Harfield handed a neatly hand-written form and put it into my two neat, clean, and manicured hands.

"So, still waiting on Grimshaw and what he knows." I added before reading aloud. "'I, Olly Grimms, hereby swear that my wife Samantha Grimms became like this through no doing from me. She slipped and hit her head. Not sure what to do with her as she has no parents and we have only married one week.

I brought her here as I am away on business for one week and will be back 24th March to see if you have made any progress.' Do you think he will be back? Maybe James and John you can go there after the visit to Uncle Danvers?"

I looked up to the Doctor, who nodded. "He promptly paid the forty guineas," He stated, "signed the form and left. We did not know how old she was or anything else about her and until I went to her room with your brother, I did not know how to proceed. It was Collins, my assistant, who suggested Mr Singh. And forgive me, I'm surprised it worked."

"No need, I get that a lot." Replied Mr Singh. "There's nothing special or magical about it. Applied science that can explain it better than I. I just know how, not the why."

"Yes. I've heard of this. Hypno suggestion, or hypnosis," I told them. "It has been around for centuries especially in other eastern countries. Once you have calmed the patient's agitation and they find your voice soothing and they relax, the state is like being asleep with your eyes open. Therefore, while in this state, any suggestion on a subconscious level the patient will obey or reply to. Did you say it worked on my cousin, Mr Singh, and can you do it again while she is asleep? Could you get her to talk more and tell us how she got to this stage?"

"I can try."

"James, Doctor Harfield, would you watch over her and attend her if necessary while I'm down here?" Both my brother and the doctor gave a nod. They left with Mr Singh.

"Hope we are not pushing too hard?" I suddenly thought, maybe she just need rest.

"Or she doesn't start screaming the place down." Put in Mags.

"That too." I added. "My father needs no more upset."

"What do you want me to do now?" asked Steven.

"John wants you to watch over us, but we need answers." They looked shocked again. "If it is against the family, then a soldier or two might act as a deterrent, especially coming here."

They looked ill at ease, but the shock was wearing off, and Mags told her husband not to be away too long tomorrow. He nodded.

"Also," I nodded, "no one goes out alone, always two." I settled back and began writing notes into Pete's journal as we waited for James to return. It was still quiet upstairs.

Later, I walked to the long garden window and thought a turnaround it would be most welcome in the light from the house. I need this, I thought as I stepped outside. Suddenly, I had an escort. "John." I inclined my head, acknowledging his presence. My heart gave a flutter.

"Catherine," he returned. "Hope you are not going far?"

"No, just a few steps, keeping well in the light. Objections?" I smiled teasingly.

"None," he said in the same vein, "as long as I can see you?"

"Well, I'm right here?" I spoke, giving him a grin.

"Miss Catherine Brentwood, I believe you are flirting with me."

"Oh Contreras, Oh Capitano, surely not." I laughed, but did little more as my dress states, I am still in mourning.

"Catherine, would you ride out with me tomorrow after your brother and I return from your uncle's? With your brother, if he will."

My heart was thudding as I looked up into his eyes. "If my brother agrees, then maybe I would. I shall ask him tonight after dinner."

James, though preoccupied with our cousin's health and her file, said later. "A fine man and I'll gladly escort you, but why, he never seemed…?"

"Interested?" I supplied. He nodded. "Maybe because I kept my distance?" I offered as an explanation, "With so much to scramble into the last six month and with father's illness, grandpa's will to deal with as Granma Ellen wasn't capable or now John is ready to retire from the army, he can think of such things. A girl would be very lucky to have Lord Melton for a husband." I added, giving John one of his grandfather's titles.

"Lord Melton," exploded James, "but he owns half of Nottinghamshire."

I nodded with a smile. "He doesn't use that title as much as Captain and his parents like me after all. I am a daughter of Lord Peter Brentwood Senior, Doctor to the Court of Queen Victoria and Chair of the Medical Board. I'm prestigious enough for even a prince, but I'll settle for a handsome Lord instead." One curt laugh escaped, as all females are taught to do when in mourning. But enough to let my brother know of my interest in Captain John Beckett, two Ts.

CHAPTER SEVEN

Visit to a Cousin

James Brentwood

Leaving early the next morning, early enough that it still had a cold tinge to it, made me pull my collar up on my lambswool coat. I drove the carriage myself, with John sitting beside me as I made my way around the Thames and out towards Essex. "How many houses has my cousin got?" I exploded after three attempts at trying to locate him.

"Well, from what I know of him," John said, "he seems to own half of London's Whitechapel, though I know that's not the case, but it's certainly a good portion of it. He is some big wig in Westminster and retired early from the army. Yet, I've not been able to discover why. He married Annabel Johnson, second cousin to your mother, though I did not know of your relations until yesterday. Grimshaw also has Johnson as a middle name, so, can't be a coincidence."

"My grandfather, General James Johnson, was a desk officer ever since taking a bullet in 1829 during the Greek Independence war of 1821 to 1832. He had five brothers, two also joined the army. One, being Annabel's father, though we have had no contact with him for a few years, never came to grandpa's funeral either. There's one in the navy, another became a soap-maker with an inherited factory from his wife's family, another I believe was a banker, the eldest which was great uncle Mason inherited the family fortune, which wasn't that great to be honest and then there were two daughters. My great aunts, Mirabella and Martha. Both outlived their third husbands and doing well on the Rummy scene. The banker has two sons and a daughter. Harry, the naval officer invested his wife's inheritance and lost a packet I believe. Story goes she never forgave him. But Mirabel, my cousin, treats his daughter Joanna as a sister. Annabel's father was the other army officer Thomas' younger son, Mayfield Johnson, but I'm sure his wife was Victoria, so I know no one called Maureen Johnson who married a Grimshaw. But my great uncles died early, so she could have married again and changed her name or used a middle name. Also, I suppose Great Grandpa Johnson could have had other siblings."

I slowed down as we entered the gates of a large old house and let out John, who hurried into the trees then bushes as he made his way around the back to the stables. I pulled up against the large grey painted door and stepped out of the rig to ring the doorbell. Straightening my coat, I pull the bell cord to announce my arrival.

A small coloured boy around seven or eight opened them and held out a silver tray, to which I left a card upon it. He invited me in and led me to a small sitting room close to the entrance. The decor left a lot to be desired, and it was gory. I did not sit down but stood by the window that looked out into the stables. John, I saw, had just slipped into the carriage house and disappeared from view as the door to the sitting room opened and Annabel herself entered, though flounced would have been a better word.

"Mr Brentwood, how nice. Though my husband is away from home, please sit and I'll do my best to entertain you in his absence. Please forgive our absence from your brother's funeral, and accept our condolences on your loss, but this is my first day up since having that wretched bug."

I gave her my thanks to her condolences and told her Samantha, her daughter sends her best wishes, but sad news she has also fallen victim to the flu as well.

"What?!" she exclaimed almost falling off her seat. "Oh dear," she suddenly changed. "I was wondering what was keeping her from home?"

"Not to worry?" I said soothingly, keeping the charade going. "She is in the care of my sisters and after a few days, she too should be back on her feet and I'll see my cousin safely back to her home."

"Thank you, Mr Brentwood. Most appreciated, I'm sure."

Just then I glimpsed John at the window, and I wound up this informative, yet distasteful visit. “Please send a message, if you take a turn for the worse, Lady Danvers.”

“Oh, thank you. Yes, I will. Please give my daughter my best wishes and a speedy recovery.” And with that, she showed me the door. I gave myself a mental shake. It was like being in a snake’s lair. Most distasteful.

I climbed aboard the Brougham and moved off at a slow pace as I waited to make sure the double doors were firmly closed, and John could climb aboard at the corner of the house hopefully without being seen.

The ride back was interesting. John had spoken to a Moneyash, a footman who spoke eloquently about Samantha and the Danvers, especially for a five-pound note.

John explained, “Moneyash said it wasn't he who had hit the girl, but he saw Captain Grimshaw, under orders from ol’ ‘arry himself step out behind her. The girl had turned when the bush at the side of the stable rustled and Grimshaw stepped out. She saw him and fainted, hitting her head on the lowered carriage canopy. He wore a look the footman did not like, and he knew then that he would not be taking the girl to her cousin’s house. He said his fear mounted as the man reached out and grabbed her roughly, dragging her out of the carriage and took her to his waiting rig.”

I nodded, then shook my head. “Annabel,” I told him, “almost fell from her chair when I told her that Samantha was with us and recovering from the flu, which apparently Lady Annabel was recovering from herself. It was her excuse for them not attending the funeral. I didn't believe a word of it. I believe they ensconced Samantha in Hanley, but I can't fathom out why, unless to keep the girl away from us." I added, before I explained, "I'll put the Brougham away and exchange it for the open top and hopefully Catherine will be ready for our turnaround Hyde."

"Thank you, James."

"Thank you, John."

All heads turned as the carriage carrying the two Brentwoods and a Captain Beckett into their direction as they entered Hyde Park that afternoon. Catherine was still dressed in black but being blond it only highlighted her beauty rather than diminishing it and John certainly looked pleased with himself. The hour passed quickly, and I had Gordon take us home. I helped my sister out, and she led us both back into the house, while the driver drove the carriage towards the stables.

Once inside we found Margaret in a tis about her brother. Apparently, no one had seen him or his Chief Inspector since Sunday. None of the constables that had gone along to a club in Queen Street had seen anything. They just never came out, the men reported. They searched the place, but the two police officers of CID had apparently vanished. All police forces were on high alert and Bow Street was looking into any cases they were on to see if they could lead to them. We will inform family as soon as we know anything. Steven told them where the family was staying at present and had left the station.

"Seems things are heating up. Are they connected; do you think?" I asked, looking at all those in the room. "Well, there's a connection with a club in Queen Street, that's for sure." I added.

"Could be," said my sister. "We need to know what Gregory was working on?"

"A case from last year," supplied Mags, handing a sheet entitled Police Report. She told us what it said. "It's about a murderer named Batho, who walked away because of sloppy police work from my brother's predecessor, who resigned from the force in the middle of the case and no one has seen him since. My brother has been having nightmares about the case, hence the R and R at home in Devon. I've been trying to reach him, but no luck. Mother has not heard from him either."

"Anyone you know on the police force that could help and keep us informed?" my sister asked.

"Sergeant Paul Taylor, he's the desk sergeant at the station. If Andy will take me, I could ask officially and get a quick word with Paul before leaving." Mags said, as she looked at her husband. "Must send a message off to mother too."

I knew that because of Mag's mother being an invalid, moving her was impossible. So, Mags and her brother represented the family, though Gregory never arrived. It was now Wednesday, and Mags had been passing messages back and forth to Devon since he never showed.

We waited for the Catford's to return. Mags started talking as soon as she got through the room's door. "I persuaded Paul to let me have a copy of my brother's case. I cannot let on otherwise he'll lose his job, but I said we need all hands on if we are to find my brother. He agreed, but if we could ignore any of his involvement, he'd be grateful."

I nodded. "Maybe Gregory left a copy here, so he could catch up with some work after the funeral on his way to the Station," and as I read it, "to see if there were any clues to his disappearance," I smiled. Mags smile matched mine.

After dinner, I saw my sister take a turn around the garden. I got close but stayed inside the room to watch. John led Catherine to the walkway around the house but stood in full view of those in the sitting room. Our parents had joined us for a few moments after dinner.

"I want to hold you close," John smiled into her eyes, keeping his distance. "There were times in the last few days, I had thought that you had taken a lot on concerning your brother and not giving yourself time to grieve. It was almost unbearable. Catherine, please will you do me the honour of becoming my wife? And let me help?"

"It would honour me to be Mrs John Beckett," my sister replied.

"Will you allow me to speak to your father to ask for your hand?"

I watched as she nodded. I could see my sister's happiness shine through.

"Are you sure?" John asked as he tilted up her face to his.

“If you'll have me. I am a very independent lady.”

He laughed, “Don’t you think it should be the other way around.”

Later, as they came in, I smiled, “Sorry, I overheard and…”

“A spring wedding,” exclaimed my father suddenly, when I stepped back into the sitting room to allow them to enter.

“Perfect.” He shook John's hand. “My sons speak highly of you, my dear chap.” My father's smile widened.

“Two weddings, two weeks apart. Don't steal my thunder,” laughed Steve as he picked me up before doing the same with Samantha. They knew each other well enough over the years, and Samantha's smile said it all. I knew, but her parents did not.

“Well, bless my soul. Then double the celebrations all round,” smiled my father, who seems very pleased. Congratulations circled the room.

Cards and music were for the night, though the music picked was all sombre themed. “The weddings, though, must be a year after the funeral.” Stated my father. The four concerned all nodded.

CHAPTER EIGHT

Taken - A Surprise Awaiting

22nd March 1849

Catherine Brentwood Writing in Peter's Journal

The next morning, after seeing Samantha had breakfast and other things, I went downstairs for my own. My parents and the elder guest were having breakfast upstairs in the dayroom and the others had all left on their errands. Things certainly went forward last night, I thought. My stomach churned at the thought of marriage. So, I had some toast and tea and thought through all I had learned. I was almost finished when Finley, the under butler, approached and coughed. I gave him permission to approach. He placed a silver tray before me with a letter on it that wasn't franked and softly said, "I found it in the hall, not a few moments before and brought it straight to you, Miss."

"Thank you," I said as I opened it. There was

no seal, so I became curious, but it turned out to be from Steven. He had found something in the small gazebo in the larger garden, and I should take a look. I thanked the under butler again and waved him away before rising. Then hurried out to the side door and into the family's garden before taking the path through the trees and beyond into the larger garden. Wondering what could Steven have found?

I arrived at the old stone building that was older than the history of the house and called "Steven!" But strangely, I received no reply.

Confused, I ventured in further and felt the sharp pain in my head before I fell to the ground. Though I did not lose my senses, I believe I was picked up and carried, then I was put down again, though not gently. I opened my eyes a little to see a tall, well-built man who had the bearing of a soldier opening the back gate. A shadow hovered close by. My stomach tightened; I had walked neatly into a trap.

I was then picked up again. They carried me for a while and I knew if I called out, it might be my last sound. My head throbbed as I fought to stay conscious. The sound of footfalls on gravel reached my ears, and I knew we had left by the back gate that should have been locked and into the back road. I kept my eyes closed. A neigh of a horse was close and then they placed me on a leather seat. I could smell the polish of beeswax. The movement of a carriage made my insides worse, and I knew I was being taken somewhere else. But I had no clue where or by whom? How did they get into the back garden and what was I going to do? What were they going to do to me? Fear stung my mind.

Voice one said, "Are you mad!? We were supposed to watch." A Londoner for sure.

A second voice answered, the accent I could not place "Yeah well, I saw an opportunity, and I took it."

"Ol' man's going to be pissed." Said the first voice, "and I need this job."

"Yeah, you'll keep it. The boss will give him a hard time and shut him up. Besides, it will take the heat off us."

I passed out and awoke to the voices. I stayed silent trying to gather information, not knowing how long I was unconscious for.

"And the coppers, thank God neither of them died. Batho went too far with the other one. I did not sign up for this, that sergeant dying was too much, not to mention that Whitehall bloke. Boss should not have signed off on that. Box or no box, wasn't worth it."

I kept quiet. *Batho killed a police officer, but the others are okay, Gregory and his boss?*

"You're wrong about the box, worth a bloody ransom, I heard." The other said.

The carriage stopped; It stood still, and I felt my head pounding, and I felt nauseous. Hoping that I did not lose my breakfast, I gritted my teeth against the feeling.

"Get her upstairs and leave her be. Boss said no touching. I'm going to check on our other guests," ordered the second voice.

Someone more than one, as he said, guests. The police, I assumed, could they help? Relief flooded through me at the thought.

Next, I was picked up again, fireman style looking the way we had come and carried through a door. I could smell beeswax cleaner, silver polish and sandalwood soap from his clothes as he took me up some stairs, though not wide ones like home, then down a narrow passageway. We entered a doorway and then I was dropped unceremoniously onto a bed, which I hoped was clean. I grunted, but I kept my eyes closed. If I don't see, I can’t say, I thought. But my captor was already walking away.

I heard the door close and then the click of the lock. I waited and listened, wondering where I was, but I moved too quick, and the darkness took me.

I awoke to find myself in a strange room, but my head thumped, and I was nauseous again. My memory was blank of how I got here. It was then my mind played tricks on me. I saw Pete, standing by a window, but it couldn’t be, I was dreaming. The darkness took me again.

I opened my eyes to find a room I’d thought I’d dreamt. I wondered how I got here and as my memory slowly returned, I saw a shadow moved across the light and I looked to the figure by the window.

“For the love of God, Pete, you gave me a scare.”

“Sorry, sis. How are you feeling?” He came over and sat on the bed. I pulled him into a hug.

“Geez, I’ve missed you,” I said tearfully. “Okay, but how did you know how to find me, and there are others here too. What gives? Why the elaborate plan to be dead?”

"It has been six weeks since I 'died' or rather someone stabbed me. I'm sorry you and everyone had to go through this, but everyone had to believe I was dead." He paused and looked back to the window.

"Well," I prompted, "why?"

"What? Oh yes, well, there was this conspiracy against the throne. Someone was going to try to kill the Queen."

"Oh my god." I said, bringing my hand to my mouth. "All of this because of a potential assassination."

"Yeah, well, that wasn't the worse, someone killed our grandfather because he got too close. He did not die of natural causes or on the battlefield. Someone poisoned him."

"Dear Lord, and the person, you were following, Grimshaw, he knew the who, what, where and the when, I suppose?"

Pete was taken aback. "You seem to be clued in. I'm amazed."

"I don't know why, once James and I found your journal and it says a lot without saying much. But the guys and I put most of it together. Did you know our cousin Harry was involved?" He nodded. "He signed off on Grimshaw's Captaincy. John found that out." I finished.

"Really, no, I had got nowhere this side of the pond, but abroad I found out that Grimms set up two men's deaths in India and started the latest war in Kandy, which cost the new king and his brothers their lives, not to mention their prime Ministers as well. They wanted to rule Sri-Lanka, or the EIC did.

He was working with the Malaysians and a European. I did a drawing of him in my first journal that vanished out of my tent and I'm not sure who he works for. He was the one who stabbed me. I made sure I hid the other in grandfather's secret pouch, which I had stitched inside my kit bag. There was no way anyone knew about it, but me and James. Grandfather gave it to me in his will and told me if I find anything useful, to put it in there."

"So, it was grandpa that recruited you?"

He nodded. "But why is James looking into 'my death'? He should have started…"

"The board extended his leave along with father's because of 'your death,'" I interjected.

"Oh, I see. And how is father and James doing?"

"Father is not doing too well and James, well, he's taking up working with the crazies. His first case sort of dropped in his arms, you might say. Someone kidnapped Samantha and we are still not sure if it involved her parents putting her in Hanley or not. We believe so but proving the matter might be hard."

"Really. Poor girl, but she's okay?" I nodded. "Well, I would put nothing past cousin Annabel, she's a nasty woman for sure and if anyone ought to be in there, it's her. Not sure about Harry, he's just plain nasty. Uncle to Grimshaw of course, whose just as nasty." He got up and winced. "Damn it hurts." As he placed a hand on his side.

"So, it was not all an act then?" I saw the paleness of his face and how he had lost weight.

"No, sis, it was not an act. I had to think fast as

I was losing a lot of blood, but lucky for me, old Trentham was on duty in the infirmary and patched me up. Killed me off and had me shipped out before the big wigs turned up. They took me straight to the airport, planed and shipped to St Bartholomew's Hospital, under an assumed name. Only a few people new my real name and it took three weeks to get back on my feet. Then it was the questions. Brass listened, debriefed me and released me this morning after I was told you had gone missing. Someone was watching the house it seems. I then went to the Manhattan club that doubles as a sewer's office or the EIC's and waited. Grimm showed up, and I followed him back to a house on Gorman Street. I sent a coded message to Andy via the next street post office boys club requesting for him and the guys to arrive and raid the place this afternoon. Sneaking around was the simple part until I surprised Grimm and we had a set to. He caught me a good one on the side and winded me, an easy target. I woke up in the hallway, and they shoved me in here, where you were being held. Thankfully you were still unconscious, and I hoped to whisk you out of here before anyone could whisper 'scandal.' They said I'd have to double up."

"So, they have two for two then." I shook my head as I gave a tight smile. Wondering if we'll ever go home.

"Not quite sis, it's six for six. I managed a quick look about. The door was easy to unlock, and I found Gracie and Jillian, cousins of Daniel, but married now, along with Gregory and his chief inspector as well. I even know who Euro is, goes by the name of Marshall, though he's a Swede and what he wanted, the assassination of our Queen. The EIC are getting too big"

"Busy lad then," said James from the door.

"James!" I said almost tearfully.

Pete struggled to get to his feet as our brother entered the room. "You're early, but welcome." They clasped shoulders "James,." said one.

"Pete," said the other, both emotional. "Glad, so glad you're still with us."

"Aye, so am I. But it was touch and go, there for a while. But I may not be here long, got to tell the folks, before heading back to Whitehall."

A gun went off echoing down the hallway. All three jarred at the noise moments before another entered.

"Catherine?!" John said, breaking into their moment as he came into the room, putting his gun back into his holster.

"I'm hungry. Is it time for lunch?" I finished for him, but with a smile. He held me close.

"Something I should know about?" Pete asked, raising a brow as I reached for John's hand. James answered.

Steve came running in at that moment. "Found Gregory and his chief and two women. John here shot Grimshaw. I think he's dead.

"About time," said Pete, with a sneer.

"Yeah, but he drew first and would have killed me, if John hadn't. The others need medical aid and help to get out of here."

"Okay, I'll check them out. Let's get out of here. John help Catherine, I've got Pete."

"Good, cus I'm starved," I said as John put an arm around my waist and helped me towards the door. I shivered, but not from cold.

Pete laughed shakily, making his long hair shake around his lean face. "You really just had to mention food." He had certainly lost weight and I'm not sure long hair suited him either.

Outside awaited three covered carriages. James took the reins as I stepped in with help. John got in behind me and then Pete, who had wanted to go somewhere else, but James ordered him inside. I recognised the two women who came out the door and were ushered into the carriage behind ours. Then Gregory made his way out, helping an older man, his Chief, I guess. He looked in a bad way. Steven, Davis, and Andy followed. James moved off, and I sat back in John's arms, feeling the warmth. James reached under his seat and pulled a rug out, and John wrapped it around me.

"We will soon have you home."

"Yes, go through Hyde. Show all we are fine." I instructed. James obliged.

Steven cantered off towards Westminster to deliver our cousins home and Davis to Bartholomew's with the detectives. Andy ran a few streets to inform the police.

We reached our destination without mishap, but as we made our way upstairs, we turned as Andy arrived with Steven and the footman handed Andy a message. He opened it and laughed. We all looked at him.

"Later," he said.

Just then, a knock came to the great oak front

doors.

"We are not expecting anyone?" said James, but as soon as Steven opened it, in rushed Colonel Harry Danvers into the hallway.

The hallway was also filling up with Davis who had just returned and Mags, who came out of the sitting room. John walked towards me as James walked closer to Harry.

"Where's your father?" He demanded loudly.

James was magnificent. "My father's not well. You will deal with me!" He announced with a touch of aggressive authority as he pointed a finger at the man.

"I will not! I will speak only to your father." Came the harsh reply.

"Then turn your fat ass and take your leave, sir, for I deal with my father's affairs now."

Danvers then looked at Pete. "Your dead!" He exclaimed snidely.

Pete spoke softly, but with contempt I had never heard before.

"The report of my demise was sadly inaccurate. The marvels of modern medicine and a good doctor. And I'm home. No thanks to your man and your orders, or are you taking them as well?" His voice became cold as he spoke.

The anger boiled in Danvers and he went almost white. Livid, I believe, was the term. "What do you accuse me of?" He flustered.

James answered, "You know very well, sir. Now, unless you have an explanation for your antics concerning your daughter, my sister and my brother, not to mention two detectives and the death of a third, I think you had better leave, or I will arrest you in my grandfather's name, and if you had anything to do with his murder, I will let you swing and I will carry out my threat to have you arrested." He said the last through gritted teeth.

"But you, but," Harry Danvers stammered, "I did nothing. You have my daughter?" It was more of an accusation than a question.

"Who will be safe in my care until I," which he emphasised, "deem fit she can travel. The flu, as you know, is deadly if not treated right, as my sister can attest too. It can almost be lethal."

"Yes, yes, absolutely right." He recovered quickly. "May I attend to my daughter next week? I'm glad that she is receiving the proper care and that both your brother and sister are gaining their feet also?"

"We will keep you posted on her recovery," James said stiffly. "I will also give my father, your best wishes and wish him a speedy recovery on your behalf as well. Maybe your wife will be on her feet in a couple of weeks and we can hold a family meeting to wish my sister, a happy birthday and on her betrothal to our family friend, Lord Melton. We will announce the betrothal on Saturday along with my brother, Steven's to your daughter, as long as there are no more upsets to delay their happy nuptials." He gave the man a questionable look.

Cousin Harry coughed at the second betrothal, but again recovered quickly. "No, let's hope everything from here on runs smoothly." He mumbled his goodbyes. Harry looked as though he was about to have a heart attack again as he turned and staggered out the door to his carriage.

“You wouldn't have arrested him?” I cried, trying to stop laughing as the door closed. “That would have been a scandal.”

“I know, but he was too flustered to realise that, but the police are a different matter.” Replied James, leading us into the sitting room. “I need a drink!”

CHAPTER NINE

The Conclusion by Catherine and James Brentwood

That night after supper, I sat watching the men in the room, as they fell back into their easy comradeship, as though the last six weeks had not happened.

"James, tell me what happened. How did you find me?" I asked, sitting next to my brother Peter, on the settee.

"James to the rescue." Said John, when James was silent, but prompted he began.

"Mags here, found out her brother was missing so, she went to the station and brought back a copy of the file Gregory was working on as you know. I asked where you were, and that footman came saying you had gone to the old gazebo in the large garden early this morning showing me the letter that Steven supposedly written."

"But it was his writing," I stated.

"No, but an excellent forgery. We went out to find you, but we already knew you weren't there.

We came back and read through the report and realised that Gregory and his boss had gone to the Queen's public house, a cover for the sewers department, or the EIC. The police were next to useless. So, John sent a message to the Barracks by runner and half a dozen men on R and R arrived and we headed off to the pub. They took a few ladies (Guns) with us and when they spoke, everybody listened, even their presence had an effect. In this case, just being present was enough for them to turn to Jelly. Squaddies turning a bar inside out, not a new thing apparently."

I laughed.

"Unheard of," said John. We all laughed too.

"Hm," said James.

I don't think he got the joke as he continued.

"Well, we found the secret passage that led down to Hogs Street, while the barman was already stating he knew nothing about the cops, who were missing and told Bow Street so yesterday. I don't think I would have believed him if he told me anything true. Davis grabbed him as I grabbed a younger man who was sitting at the bar. A canary, or a pair, I believe was the term, and they sang so sweet, because I was in no mood to listen to anything else. I put my doctor aside. Today, I was a brother. Besides, John was about to make Swiss cheese out of them all."

Pete laughed again. "You were in fine form then, brother, but where does the rescue fit in? And my letter told you all about the house on Gorman Street."

"What letter?" James asked surprised.

"This one!" said Andy, pulling the letter out of his pocket.

"Post office runners, I should have found a Bow Street Runner," complained Pete. No one laughed.

"Okay, enough," I stated, "let's get on with it."

James nodded and began again. "John waved a rifle at all in the room, but thankful no one looked close at the empty chamber. We wanted information, not arrested by Bow Street. Anyway, we were told to go to a house on Gorman Street, Whitechapel. Well, they gave me an address, and we left, followed by my army and we surrounded the place. Once inside, we searched the place. John here, came across Grimshaw, who put up some resistance, and tried to shoot Steve. John shot him instead. So, with Grimms dead, the European captured, who was hiding upstairs, but he was unconscious when we left, thanks to Davis and not long after the police arrived, and he's now behind bars for the attempted assassination of Queen Victoria, and will soon sing about all others involved, hopefully including Danvers. So, all's right with the world. The fancy box, they had, I was told by Gregory was an early nineteenth century tea box made by the Eastern India Company worth only a few bob, but it seemed they were looking for the original that belonged to Thomas Becket and was worth a fortune, but no one knows where it is."

"I do," said John. "A family heirloom, but it's empty, sorry."

"Well, that seems to close that mystery then."

I was to be given the real one as a wedding

present from Lord Melton, and the other which was given to me by Gregory, but was given to Samantha instead, who had taken a liking to it and as it did not mean the same to me as it did to her, I let her have it. She was going to be as close to me as Mary was, so my first gift of many, I was sure." She smiled as she looked at me.

"I sent a letter to mother," she told us, "And told them of my wish to marry Steven, yet they have not replied."

"And the man that hit me?" I enquired.

"Well, John took care of him apparently, he was a footman of Harry's." I thanked him.

"My pleasure," he replied with the returned smile.

"Danvers is up to his thick neck in this whole affair. I knew it," said James, "but he will be dealt with by the palace presently and quietly, I'm sure, because of Samantha. How far in this was his wife was anyone's guess, but the lady, it was said, due to ill health, will probably retire to the country, but forever under house arrest." He concluded.

How much, I thought, *both my brother, James and her husband to be, Steven wanted to tell Samantha was up to them. I hope they realised Samantha was not me and her fragile mind may not grasp the full extent of her parents' treachery. They would allow her a controlled visit, I'm sure to see her mother at least once a month, but when her father would be allowed to visit also, apparently with the Queen's blessing, would be up to the Palace discretion.*

EPILOGUE

The Night of a Thousand Lights

The following Saturday in the evening, we were all ready. And as I glided down the stairs, I saw the look on John's face, and I realised I loved him with all my heart. I was a very fortunate female. He collected me as I stepped off the last step.

"I was wrong," he whispered, "about there being no Becket's treasure. I think I found the missing treasure, that's right under my nose. I am a very fortunate man indeed. Catherine Lucinda Brentwood, Beckett's Treasure. Now, there's a title." I dropped him a curtsey for the compliment as he laughed.

The night of the thousand lights was waiting, the theme for tonight's ball that was to be held in a garden of the first minister, Lord Melbourne and he would not take no for an answer.

We gathered in the hallway.

"If we are all ready," beamed James proudly before he turned to the door to lead us to the three carriages and, as if by slow motion, I watched my brother leave the house first. Then Mags and Andy, Davis followed to the third carriage. Steven helped Samantha down the steps and Peter followed them to the second, the newly returned son and brother. I would follow with Lord Melton to step into the first with James.

On the doorstep, I looked up at John. "Okay?" He smiled. I nodded, before looking back and that was the picture that I wanted to carry in my heart forever. There were our parents standing in the hall, watching as we departed for the night's festivities. My mother and father and my younger sister, standing at the bottom of the stairs looking at me and all had tears on their faces.

'Happiness comes in short measures,' I heard my brother Peter say behind me. Here, tonight, I had a glassful.

"Happiness is family," Pete whispered in my ear, "keep it close Katie, always keep us close!"

I knew I would as I closed the journal for good.

THE END

ABOUT THE AUTHOR

Anita started writing back in the early 1990s when she was diagnosed with fibromyalgia and her first novels have taken over twenty years to write. She loves writing and hopes it continues long into the future with plenty more adventures for her characters. She says, Fibromyalgia does not hold me back; if I can, I will. Anita lives in Nottingham, Great Britain, and enjoys visiting new places, meeting new people and visiting family. Follow her at: https://www.facebook.com/anita.mills.33
Or on amazon: https://www.amazon.com/Anita-Blakeman-Mills/e/B097RVZK1R

From the Author:

Thank you for choosing this book. If you enjoyed it, please consider telling your friends or leaving a review on Amazon, Goodreads or the site where you bought it. Word of mouth is an author's best friend, and it is much appreciated.

Anita K Mills.

OTHER BOOKS

<u>The Chronicles of Tralia</u>

Book 1: The Sorceress of the Five Crowns

<u>A Debutant's Mystery</u>

Book 1: Beckett's Treasure

Thanks June

I hope you enjoy

my email is

anitamills@live.co.uk

if you would be so kind

to leave me a review

all the best

Anita Mills

Printed in Great Britain
by Amazon

63575418R00069